SECRETS
OF
THE
MUSEUM

D1716736

SECRETS
OF
THE
MUSEUM

A Novel

Roy Carl Weiler Sr.

iUniverse, Inc.

New York Lincoln Shanghai

SECRETS OF THE MUSEUM

iUniverse books may be ordered through booksellers or by contacting:

iUniverse
2021 Pine Lake Road, Suite 100
Lincoln, NE 68512
www.iuniverse.com
1-800-Authors (1-800-288-4677)

Because of the dynamic nature of the Internet, any Web addresses or links contained in this book may have changed since publication and may no longer be valid.

This is a work of fiction. All of the characters, names, incidents, organizations, and dialogue in this novel are either the products of the author's imagination or are used fictitiously.

ISBN: 978-0-595-47718-0 (pbk)
ISBN: 978-0-595-71660-9 (cloth)
ISBN: 978-0-595-91980-2 (ebk)

Printed in the United States of America

* FOR MOM *

ACKNOWLEDGMENTS

I am indebted to quite a few people for their help, patience and kindness that made this book possible. I have taken artistic license with some of the history and information but have tried to keep this work as true to the real world as possible. Any and all mistakes are mine. It is a work of fiction after all. My special thanks to my friend and editor, Annina Lorna Anton, my Aunt Marie Weiler, other friends who first read and commented so helpfully during and after the writing of this book, and most especially to The Egg Harbor City Historical Society.

ONE

Cynthia Dobbs was dying. All of modern medical science couldn't help her. It talked a good game but the fact was that at her last treatment Dr. Hicks had told her, "I hate to say this but you only have a short time left—if you're lucky, maybe a year. The treatments are no longer slowing the progress of the disease. If there is a bright side, there's a chance that the test results due next week will show that it hasn't spread to your liver." He leaned back in his old office chair, and smiled sadly at her. "Now ... you won't really feel much pain, aside from the short episodes you have been having, until just before the end. The pain medications I have prescribed should be effective for most of the time remaining to you. I'm so sorry Cynthia. What are you going to do? What plans have you made? We both knew this was coming for some time."

She sat up straighter in her seat and said. "Well, this may surprise you doctor, but I'm going to go to Egg Harbor City—that's in New Jersey—and research my family history. There are stories my grandmother told about a doctor who lived there at the end of the nineteenth and into the early twentieth century. She said he could cure almost anything. He did strange and wonderful things with the cedar waters from the local swamps."

"Be very careful my dear. There have been many people that I've seen chasing after herbal and mystical cures when they are dying. Don't get your hopes up. Things like that are only fantasies, offering false hopes. Get your affairs in order and let medical science make you as comfortable as possible until the end. Don't go chasing after old wives' tales."

"I'm sorry Dr. Hicks, but I'm not ready to lie down and die. I come from a long line of fighters and I won't give up without a fight. There's a museum in Egg Harbor City in one of the buildings old Dr. Smith had as part of his cedar water sanatorium and treatment center. I'm going there and try to find a cure that your modern science can't provide, unless you have something new that we haven't tried. I will use the time that remains to find anything that might save me."

With that she left Dr. Hicks' offices and headed for her mother's house. She had been slowly cleaning it out since her mother's death two years before. Just yesterday she had come across a packet of old letters from Egg Harbor City written by her grandmother in the 1950's. The family had lived in Egg Harbor City for almost a hundred years—before she and her mother had moved away to Glenfalls twenty years ago—when Cynthia was only 19.

As she drove up to her mom's house she could see that the front door was standing open. Parking her car in the driveway she thought, 'I know I closed and locked it when I left.' As she walked up to the door, it suddenly banged shut in a strong gust of October wind. The leaves rustled around her feet and she felt the autumn chill like the cold hand of death that had been reaching for her since she was diagnosed with SA.

She got a grip on her nerves, opened the door and stepped into the foyer. Her heart jumped into her throat as a large gray cat raced out the door past her. She recognized Bootsie, Mrs. Hurley's cat from next door. As her heart settled back in place there was a crash from the back of the house. Now angrier than frightened, she yelled. "Is someone in here?" as she stomped down the hall, flicking on lights as she went. She arrived in the kitchen at the back of the house just in time to watch through the big bay window as someone ran out the backyard gate. The back door was closed, but one of the windowpanes was broken, and the tall planter that always stood next to the back door lay smashed on the floor. Obviously that was the source of the noise she had heard. Whoever it had been must have knocked it down in their hurry to get out.

She called the police and was standing outside the front door thirty minutes later when the Glenfalls police finally arrived. They searched through the house and took her statement. When she asked why someone would break in the back and then open the front door, they told her whoever it was might have looked out the front or let someone else in that way and then not closed the door tightly, afterward the wind could have blown it open. If she had no other questions, she could pick up a copy of the police report for insurance purposes the next afternoon. And not to worry. In their opinion, it was just kids.

The afternoon was coming to a close, with heavy dark clouds that made it look as though it might snow. Cynthia thought it felt like snow too. She decided to have a cup of hot tea to settle her nerves before cleaning up the broken mess and getting some work done.

After her tea, Cynthia cleaned up the broken things and taped a piece of cardboard over the broken window. Just as she finished, a wind-driven mix of snow, sleet and rain began to pound the house. She decided to start a fire in the fireplace and stay the night. She checked that all the doors and windows were locked, then sat in the living room by the fire and started on the stack of letters her grandmother had written all those years ago.

She was surprised to find an additional letter stuffed into the thick envelope from 1955. The other letter was much older and mailed from New York City in 1906. It was from her great grandfather, Max Schnee, confirming a reservation for him and his ailing wife, Emma, at Dr. Smith's health resort sanatorium in Egg Harbor City. Her great grandfather was most anxious about his wife's condition. His last line stated, 'Dr. Smith, you are my last hope to cure my lovely wife Emma.'

She gently held the old letter in trembling hands, and thought that here was the first bit of written proof of the stories her mother and grandmother had told. Emma must have been cured or her grandmother would not have been born. But what was Emma suffering from so long ago? What did Dr. Smith do to cure her? Most importantly, could it be found and would it work as a cure for Cynthia?

Hours later when the fire was about out and she had finished reading the last of the letters, there were no more clues to be found. Her tired eyes were drooping she turned out the lamp and wearily climbed the stairs to her old bedroom. Even though she had moved to her own apartment fifteen years before, she still had clothes and things here. When her mother was sick she had spent many a night with her; having her own room had come in very handy.

The storm had passed and there was bright moonlight coming through the bedroom window as Cynthia slowly undressed. She gazed at her naked reflection in the full-length mirror. Her body looked young, trim, and healthy in the silvery moonlight. How could she be dying? At thirty-nine she still turned men's heads with her trim figure and full breasts. Dark hair fell across her bare shoulders— shoulders Rick had loved to kiss and touch. Rick—the thought of his leaving when she told him she was ill plus caring for her mother was still a painful memory. Yet just the thought of his touch and kisses on her skin stirred her passion even now. Closing her eyes and softly touching her breast she trembled with excitement. She slid her other hand down across the flat of her tummy to that special place. It didn't take long and she was in the grip of physical pleasure, strong memories of his touch helping to bring her nearer to a climax. Her excitement was shattered as the bedroom door creaked slowly open. Startled, she grabbed her robe and faced the door to see, what? Nothing. She turned on the overhead light and there was Bootsie. Picking up the big cat she said, "How did you get in here?" The cat purred and snuggled against her chest.

Cynthia carried the cat downstairs to the kitchen. In the refrigerator she found a small creamer from the coffee shop up the street. She poured the bit of cream in a saucer for Bootsie and put it on the floor. While stooped over she noticed a loose floorboard sticking up about an inch near the wall. On closer examination she discovered it could be lifted out easily. In the space below she found a small metal box. It was locked. Her mother had never said anything about a hidden box.

Working with a letter opener she soon had the lock broken, and lifted the lid. Inside she found a single gold coin, three more letters from 1906, and one from 1909. She sat at the table and read the letter from 1909. It was from her Great Granddad Max to someone named William. It read:

Dear William,

I don't know how we can ever thank you for your help. Just three years here in Egg Harbor under the care of the wonderful Dr. Smith and my Emma is well again. Not just well but very healthy, and pregnant! I am also sending a twenty dollar gold piece to repay with interest the loan you made to help us. Gold cannot repay nearly what I feel we owe you.

Do come visit—it has been so long since we saw you. I am doing well and am now working as a polisher in the Liberty Cut Glass Factory. We live in a nice house not far from the sanatorium. I trust that all is well with you.

Your friend, Max

The letter had been returned as undeliverable, so the coin must be the one Max had sent to William. She peered at the coin as she turned it in her hand. Yes, it was indeed a twenty dollar gold piece from 1907. But what had happened to William? Did he never get back in touch with Max? If he did why was the gold coin still here? So many questions, so few answers, and since her mother's death, no one left to ask. Perhaps she would find out the answers in Egg Harbor City.

Bootsie had finished his cream; she put him out the back door telling him, "Go home kitty!" The cat regarded her with his enigmatic cat stare for a moment, and then scampered into the garden. Cynthia stood for a few minutes in the moonlight, thinking, 'Such a beautiful clear night now that the storm has passed.' A breeze tickling her bare legs made her shiver, and her feet were getting very cold on the wet concrete step. She hurried back inside and up to bed. As she slid under the covers her thoughts turned once again to Rick. 'Why did you have to turn out to be such a jerk?' she thought as she drifted off to sleep.

*   *   *   *

Cynthia was running, running as fast as she could. A cold black hand was just grabbing hold of her. She woke in a cold sweat. The dream had left her trembling and tangled in the sheets. She sat up and looked at the bedside clock, 2 a.m. Damn! She needed some sleep but she was wide-awake now, and almost afraid to go back to sleep. Should she take one of the sleeping pills Dr. Hicks had given her? He had said they were very mild, just enough to take the edge off her upset mind. She thought 'No, I don't like drugs. I have enough drugs in me trying to fight the disease, even though I'm not going to take any more of them. They aren't working anymore anyway. I would rather have a bit of brandy and see what else is in those other letters I found.' She had been told she was allowed a small amount of alcohol without any side effects from the medications.

She donned her robe and this time a pair of slippers to keep her feet warm, and went down to the kitchen. There was a bottle of blackberry brandy in the cabinet above the sink. With a half glass of the brandy in hand she sat down at the kitchen table and taking a small sip, opened the letter dated July 1906. It was from the mysterious William. It read:

Dear Max,

I hope you and Emma are settled in at Dr. Smith's. I am sending this care of his health resort and can only hope it finds its way to you. You said you would write as soon as you arrived there, but I haven't heard from you and it is three months since you left New York. I wish I could have lent you more than fifteen dollars to help you but I just couldn't afford any more.

Please write soon and let me know you are all right, and an address so I can write to you directly.

Wishing you the best, my love to Emma.

Your friend,
William

Not much help from that one. But at least it explained the loan William had made to Max and Emma. The next letter was dated August 1906. After pouring a little more brandy in her glass Cynthia read:

Dear Max,

I was so glad to receive your letter of July twentieth. I was surprised that you said you had written in May. I never got that letter. I was happy to hear that you and Emma are settled in a rooming house on Philadelphia Avenue, and my letter had found its way to you. Don't worry about the money. I know you will pay it back when you can. You just need to get Emma well. That's the important thing. I will try to come visit next year. I have found that I can go to Philadelphia by train and get another train from there to Egg Harbor City. I was sorry to hear the trip from here to there was so difficult for you. Yet traveling with those people in their wagon was the least expensive way for you to get there, even though it took a week.

I hope you find work soon and Dr. Smith's magic waters work to cure Emma.

Always,
William

Cynthia thought, 'Magic waters—doesn't that sound wonderful? If only it would be so easy.' Taking a big yawn she said, "One more little glass of brandy and I must go to bed."

She sat back down at the table with her brandy and opened the last envelope. It was empty! How could that be? Third envelope postmarked from September 1906 and it was empty. No letter? Damn! Cynthia thought, 'Oh well. I'll take my brandy and go upstairs to bed. So tired.' Carefully climbing the stairs one at a time she made it to her bedroom, and stood swaying slightly in the doorway. She said aloud, "How much brandy did I have?" She looked at the empty glass in her hand and tried to put it on the nightstand. It thumped on the floor as she tumbled into bed.

*   *   *   *

Birds were chirping and the sun was bright in her bedroom window when Cynthia opened her eyes. "Oh, my head," she moaned. As she sat on the edge of the bed she was stabbed in the eyes by bright sunlight. She held an arm across her eyes as she walked stiffly to the window and closed the drapes. Darkness. Much better. Aspirin and a shower—that's what she needed. She shrugged out of her nightshirt, adjusted the shower and stepped into the stinging spray.

Later, dressed in jeans, a gray cable knit sweater, and a pair of comfortable old flats she went down to the kitchen for coffee and to see if there was anything she could eat for breakfast. With coffee percolating in her mom's old stove-top percolator she searched the cabinets for something to eat. She hadn't kept much of anything here since her mother's death, but luckily in the freezer she found some donuts from a few weeks ago. 'A few seconds in the microwave and TADA—breakfast.' As she was taking them from the freezer one slipped from the plastic bag, landed on the floor, and rolled under the table.

Down on her hands and knees she crawled under the table after it, where she found the missing letter. She sat on the floor and read:

Dear Max,

I was delighted to read in your letter of August 29th that your Emma is feeling much better. Dr. Smith is an amazing man like I told you he can cure almost anything. I hope to visit you sooner then I had thought, perhaps as early as this coming Christmas. It will be wonderful to see the both of you again.

It was great to hear you found work at one of the cedar mills, but Max, I'm sure you can do better than that. You are so handy with small delicate things. Lumber mills are hard, dirty, dangerous places. Be careful, and keep looking for something better.

My love to Emma. Your friend,
William

Sitting there on the floor, holding her throbbing head, she thought, 'More questions than answers as always. This Amazing Dr. Smith could cure anything, but he was dead long ago. How am I going to find his cure? Nobody else has apparently found it, or surely the world would be disease free by now.' She said to herself, "Don't despair!"

Her father, who died when she was ten, had always told her when she was playing ball, "Play to win. Run like hell. Get up if you fall." He also said. "I love you baby." He always called her his baby. She loved her dad, but he had been dead almost thirty years, and this was now, and it was she who was going to die. Getting up from the floor, she pushed the letters and things to the side of the table and sat down to donuts and coffee.

TWO

Three thirty in the afternoon, and not a single visitor to the museum. Kyle sat in the kitchen and finished his tea. He hadn't cared much for coffee since his breakup with Brenda. Two years and he still thought about her everyday. They drank a lot of coffee together. He thought. 'Might as well get ready to close—on a snowy/rainy afternoon like this, nobody is coming out to visit the Egg Harbor City Historical Museum. Small town, no interest.'

Just then the sleigh bells jangled as someone came in the front door. Kyle walked out into the museum proper and beheld one of the loveliest women he had ever seen. Long dark hair; with a great build, dressed in slacks, sweatshirt, and snow boots—with a nice smile and icy bits of melting snow in her hair.

"The wind has blown a snow angel in my door. Hi, I'm Kyle. Welcome to our museum. Please sign our visitor's book. Feel free to look around and if you have any questions just ask. I will do my best to make up an answer," he said, giving a slight bow, a big smile and a wink.

Cynthia giggled and smiled. "Do you make up all your answers to questions about the things in this museum? I'm Cynthia, and I have lots of questions." She thought he was a most striking man. Muscular, slightly taller than she, soft brown eyes, with silver-blond hair, maybe a few years older than she, but very handsome. She liked what she saw, but right now she needed information, not romance. "What can you tell me about Dr. Smith and his cedar water treatments?"

"Ah, the great Dr. Smith. Let's see. We have a display case right here by the front door containing photos of his cedar water health resort, and that's a picture of the old boy himself. When that photo was taken he claimed to be one hundred and eight years old."

"Wow, a hundred and eight! Is that true?"

"We aren't sure of his date of birth, so there's no way to tell; later in the 1920 census he reported his age as one hundred and forty-three. We do have a copy of that census sheet, and that's what it says. Who knows? He could have been any age. Just look at that picture. Doesn't he look well over a hundred?"

Cynthia stared at the little old man in the photograph with his long gray beard down to his waist, slightly bowed legs and a cane in his hand. "He certainly does look as if he could be that old. But what information do you have about his treatments? Did he really cure people of things no one else could?" A big book on display in the case was labeled, *The Doctor's Book*. "Would it be possible for me to look at that book?"

"I'm afraid not. Some of the things on display are very fragile, that book in particular. I know because it took two of us to put it in there without the pages falling out. It is literally falling apart. We couldn't let anyone handle it."

Cynthia wanted desperately to look in that book, but she said, "I can understand that; what else do you have here that was his? Or that has information about the treatments he used to cure his patients?"

"Well, let's see, we have photos of people walking in the serpentine stream. He made them walk against the current in all kinds of weather, both summer and winter. Look at this picture from 1906, patients up to their waists in the stream with snow on its banks."

Cynthia stared at the old photo of people in long woolen swimming clothes standing in the freezing water. Maybe she was wrong to think he had a cure for anything at all. Anybody with half a brain knows you don't go in swimming in January! She'd lost track of what Kyle was saying.

"… cured many people."

"I'm sorry, what did you say?"

"I was saying people came from all over to partake of the doctor's cures. He is said to have cured many people. Word is he did wonderful things with the waters from the cedar swamps around Egg Harbor City."

"But what good could walking in freezing water do anybody? Didn't they get pneumonia or something?"

"There are no written records of anyone getting sick from walking in the water. Did you notice when you drove up the serpentine stream is just across the street from the museum? It and the museum building are the only remaining structures from Dr. Smith's Health Resort."

Looking out the window of the front door, Cynthia could just make out across the street, through the snow and rain, a waterway that looped back on it self again and again. "People walked in that thing in this kind of weather? Were there shelters or buildings for them to come out of the water into and dry themselves to get warm? How could they do something like that? Brrr!"

"There were many other buildings here when the place was running at its peak. There was a windmill and a glass drying building behind where the museum is now, and over next to the serpentine was the sanatorium. Next to that was the hotel; it was built because so many people came to be cured and they had family or friends come with them. You can see part of the foundation of the sanatorium near the leading side of the serpentine, and the octagon shaped foundation from the windmill can be seen out behind the museum building."

"But was that all he did? Make the patients walk in the flowing waters? Surely he must have had other treatments?"

"Oh, he did. He made a tonic and an elixir that treated all kinds of other ailments. I think they were just water, coloring and a bit of alcohol. But who knows? It was a long time ago, and there are no written records left to say anything about it. Look I kind of hate to say this but the museum is supposed to close at four pm, and it's nearly five. Not that I don't enjoy talking to a visitor past closing, especially such a lovely and interesting one like you. However, I have a dinner engagement at six so I really must close up. Could you come back another time? If you are really interested in doing some serious research I could meet you here and open the place for you at other times than the regular hours. Are you staying in town?"

"Yes. I'm trying to get my grandmother's house open and in a livable condition. It's been boarded up for the last fifteen years. My mother was executor of her estate and never got here to clean it out and sell it. Maybe you know it? The Stanton place?"

"On Atlantic Avenue, by the railroad? Sure, everybody knows the old Stanton place. Most people say it's haunted. Have you been in there? Is it in any condition to live in?"

"I've been here for two days, and I had the electric and things turned on before I arrived. It is a bit of a mess, but livable, yes. I came here to the museum the first day I was in town, but the sign says you are only open Wednesdays and Saturdays. Then today with the rain I had to put a lot of buckets and pots around under the leaks in the roof or I would have been here sooner. Why do they say it's haunted?"

"Look," said the man in a genuinely regretful tone, "I really don't have the time to talk with you right now. I'm going to be late as it is. Could you give me a number where I can reach you later tonight or tomorrow? Maybe we can meet for lunch or something and I can tell you all about anything I know that might interest you. We could even meet here at the museum if you like."

"If you must go, you must. Please call me. Here's my card. The cell number is working here, and even late tonight would be fine. I will be up working on that old house until the wee hours I'm sure—mopping up water and things."

As he took her card he held her hand for a moment. "I will, I'll call you tonight after oh, say about eight thirty. Would that be okay?"

"Thank you so much for your help. I'm sorry to have kept you late—please do call. I'll talk to you then." With that she walked out the door into the rainy evening.

Kyle watched her walk to her car. As she got behind the wheel she waved to him. He waved back and thought, 'She's the nicest looking girl to hit this town in a long time.' He had kind of a silly grin on his face as he took in the open sign and closed the museum for the night.

When he arrived at his friend's house, Jim said, "You look like the cat that swallowed the canary. And you're never late, what's up?"

"Oh, nothing."

Jim's wife, Virginia, said, "Look at that grin! I bet he met some nice girl, and that's why he's late. Now look, he's blushing! Okay, Kyle, who is she?"

"No one! Really—well this nice looking lady came in the museum right before I closed, and had a lot of questions about Dr. Smith and the health resort and stuff. But she is rather attractive and yes, that's why I'm late. You'll never guess where she's staying!"

Jim said, "Knowing you I wouldn't be surprised if she's staying at your place." He poked Kyle in the ribs as he handed him a beer.

"I wish. But even I can't work that fast. No, she's staying at the old Stanton place." Jim and Virginia both stood still and stared at him.

Virginia said, "Does she know about that place? Did you tell her? She could be in danger!"

Jim said, "Now Genie it ain't that bad. Nothing has ever happened there that anybody knows of for sure. Just rumors and such. What did you tell her Kyle?"

"I did mention it's supposed to be haunted, but I didn't go into any details. I was already late to be here. I got a phone number for her and I might call her later. Now, Virginia what are you cookin' that smells so great?"

THREE

Cynthia stopped at the grocery store on the way home to pick up a mop, another bucket, and some lunch meat. As she left the store she saw that it had stopped raining and decided to drive past the museum to take a better look at that serpentine stream. She parked the car across from the museum and stepped out into the damp air. There was a sign on the fence: "Peace Pilgrim Park." She made a mental note to ask Kyle about that. Walking along the fence, she came to an open gate. A path led down the slope to the water. She followed the path along the stream and found a statue, picnic tables and benches. It would have been nice to sit peacefully and relax if everything wasn't wet, plus she was feeling the nip in the air.

She headed back to the car thinking, 'I have a great many things to ask Kyle.' She thought about what he had said when she entered the museum. He had called her a snow angel. He did have a nice smile, and he was certainly an attractive man. Rick had been an attractive man, but he was nothing like Kyle. Thank God.

Cynthia slid in behind the wheel and drove to her grandmothers' house. It was very dark. One of the things she had been meaning to fix was the outside light. She left the car lights on so she could see better, unlocked the side door and reached inside to turn on the lights. Instead of the light switch her hand encountered a soft squishy something. Jerking her hand back she hurried to the car for a flashlight. She returned to the door, still trembling, and looked inside. Shreds of wet wallpaper had curled down over the light switch. She breathed a sigh of relief. "Damn!"

She reached in carefully with the flashlight and flicked on the lights. The old kitchen looked sad and tired with water stains on the walls and faded wallpaper hanging down here and there. She wrinkled her nose at the smell of dampness in the air. After carrying all the things in from the car, she set to work cleaning.

Really getting into her tasks, Cynthia had most of the downstairs dried out when the cell phone chirped and made her jump. She had not realized how much time had passed. It was Kyle, and he said, "Hey lovely lady, its nine o'clock and I'm free for the rest of the night. How about a nightcap somewhere or coffee at the diner? We can talk about whatever you like, or maybe just get to be friends."

"Hey, yourself! I'm too much of a mess to go anywhere, but you could come here. I could offer a cup of coffee or a glass of wine, if you wouldn't mind the smell of dampness. You know where it is?"

"I do, and I can be there in ten minutes if that's okay. Should I bring anything?"

"All that you know about Dr. Smith and Egg Harbor City is all I need. I'll supply everything else. See you in ten?"

"You bet!" he said, and she heard the phone click. Then she thought, 'Oh my God! He's gonna be here in ten minutes, and I look like an old scrub woman!' Cynthia rushed upstairs, brushed her hair, rinsed with mouthwash, slipped out of her sweater and into a fresh blouse, dabbed some perfume on, and the doorbell rang. 'It can't be ten minutes already,' she thought as she hurried down the stairs.

She opened the door to no one. She knew she had heard the doorbell. Who could have rung it? She thought it was Kyle, but nobody was there and it had started to rain again. She closed the door and headed back upstairs, and just as she reached the bathroom the doorbell sounded again. She waited, it rang again. She went downstairs and opened the front door. Nobody there! Cynthia was just turning back inside when headlights pulled into the driveway.

Kyle got to the steps and said, "Wow, waiting at the door for me, I'm impressed."

Cynthia had to smile at his exuberance. "Not really, but the strangest thing just happened with the doorbell. Come on in. What would you like to drink?"

"Tell you the truth, coffee would be great."

Heading into the kitchen she said over her shoulder, "Coming right up. How do you take it?"

"Black is good."

"You drink it black? Me too. A couple of purists—what are the chances?" Suddenly she felt very happy and the doorbell was forgotten.

Kyle followed her into the kitchen and sat comfortably at her table. She thought he looked very much at home as she bustled around and started the coffee. While it dripped she put two mugs on the table and sat in the chair next to his. "So how long have you been volunteering at the museum?"

"Well let's see, I've been a member of the Historical Society for five years and I started doing Saturdays about two years ago. Then last year I was on the Sesquicentennial Committee; we had a big celebration that summer. Now you're here to brighten up this old town. Seems things just get better and better"

As she poured their coffee she smiled, and blushed a little. He made her feel young and attractive—if only he could make her forget her illness. "How was your dinner engagement?" she asked. "Were you terribly late?"

"No not really. It was just dinner with my friends, Jim and his wife, Virginia, at their place. Speaking of dinner, have you eaten?

"No I haven't. I got home and started right in cleaning because of all the leaks. Truth be told, I'm starving."

"Well how about we get some food into you? We could order in, Chinese, or pizza? How about it, whadya say?"

"But you've already eaten. I couldn't sit and eat with you just … watching me."

"Then, how about this? I saw the fireplace in the living room; a fire would help dry out the place, and we could order something in. Whatever we have, I can eat some. Jim and my other friends are always telling me they don't know where I put all the food without gaining a pound." He smiled and winked at her. "What about it?"

"I don't even know if the fireplace is safe. But there's wood in it and some stacked on the hearth. It has probably dry-rotted with age; it must have been there since my Gran died. If you want to try I suppose we could at least take a look at it."

Before she was even finished speaking, he was up and headed into the living room. He said over his shoulder, "These old fireplaces are great—made from the natural bog iron field stones found in this area. They are tough as anything. I'll light a piece of newspaper to see if it'll draw a draft."

By the time Cynthia got to the living room, he was on his knees in front of the fireplace sticking his head inside, looking around. She said, "I haven't cleaned the fireplace yet. Please be careful."

"Do you have a flashlight so I can look up the chimney? It's very dusty but the hearth and fire box look okay." She handed him the flashlight. He checked the damper and while looking up the chimney, said, "Looks clear."

She started to giggle. He asked, "What's so funny?"

Handing him some paper towels she said. "You look like a chimney sweep. You have soot on your face just like Dick Van Dyke in the old Mary Poppins movie." He smiled and her giggles turned to real laughter. "Now you have it on your shirt too."

"I guess I'm just a mess, but the fireplace looks okay. Can I use your bathroom to clean up? Then while you order pizza, I'll light a fire." She showed him the way to the downstairs bathroom and gave him an entire roll of paper towels. "I won't be to long. Why don't you call Pizza Palace—they're just around the block from here and they're open till midnight. They have great pizza." He gave her the number and closed the bathroom door.

She had just finished the ordering when he came back and said, "There, is this better? Except for a few smudges on my shirt I think it'll do." Before she could answer he was at the fireplace again arranging the kindling and wood. "Do you have some old newspaper to get this started?" She did and in a short time he had a nice fire going. The warm glow flickered around the room. He asked, "Did you say something about wine when I got here?"

She said, "I was just thinking the same thing—a nice glass of red wine by the fire while we wait for the pizza man. I only have Merlot, is that okay?"

"You won't believe this, but Merlot is my favorite."

"Mine too! I almost always have a bottle on hand." They laughed together. She liked the sound of his laugh—liked his deep, rich voice. She got a bottle and two glasses from the kitchen and they sat side by side on the faded carpet in front of the fire.

He took the bottle from her and said, "Screw-top—my all time favorite vintage!" Their laughter rang through the house. After filling the glasses he said quite formally, "A toast, to the lady with the beautiful eyes; may all your wishes come true!" As they clinked glasses and drank, she watched him over the rim of her glass and thought, 'His eyes are smiling for me.'

Suddenly there was a loud pop and a shower of sparks from the fireplace. A bright red ember landed on the carpet and started to smoke. He was on his feet and crushing it out under the toe of his boot before she could even jump up.

Standing next to him, looking up into his eyes she said, "You're fast!" He stared into her eyes and was leaning slightly toward her, his head tilting slowly down and just when she thought he was about to kiss her, the doorbell rang.

He moved away from her and said, "Pizza time, I guess." While heading for the door, Cynthia realized she had wanted to kiss him. She felt a little chill as she opened the door. Was it the disappointment of that missed kiss, or the cold damp wind that swept into the room? The pizza man stood there in the rain. She motioned for him to enter. He carried the box into the living room and placed it on a side table.

Kyle hurried over and gave him a twenty-dollar bill. "Keep the change, for coming out on a night like this—you deserve it, Ted."

After Ted left, Cynthia said, "You know him?"

Kyle chuckled. "Oh yes, his family has owned the Pizza Palace forever. Besides, pizza is one of the staples in my diet. Now all we need are some napkins and more wine."

"I'm afraid paper towels will have to do." Sitting down by the fire once more she opened the pizza box and Kyle started to laugh. "What's so funny?" she asked.

"You got the large supreme with everything but the kitchen sink on it. If I had ordered, it would have been the same. Are you sure you're not my long lost twin or something?"

Giggling like a schoolgirl, Cynthia could only smile and think, 'We like everything the same—how funny.' She said, "No, I'm not your long lost twin. If you haven't noticed we look nothing alike. But we certainly do seem to have the same tastes. Do you have a twin, or any siblings at all?"

His smile vanished. "I had a sister, but she died in a car crash in 1975, while I was … away on a trip. She and her boyfriend were on their way home from their senior prom."

"Oh, how awful! I'm so sorry! I … I had no idea and I didn't mean to pry."

"It's okay. It was a long time ago. Your question was just normal conversation. Let's get to this pizza before it gets cold. You know, now that its here and I smell it, you may have to fight me for your share." There was a twinkle in his eye and an easy smile on his face again.

Cynthia thought, 'Maybe not fight, but I wouldn't mind wrestling with you.' She watched his lips as he took a bite of pizza. Nice soft full lips. She asked, "Is it good?"

With his mouth full he mumbled, "Always!"

*   *   *   *

Later, with the pizza box empty, and the wine almost gone, they were leaning shoulder to shoulder on the sofa, his left arm behind her, her right arm behind him. With the fire flickering on its last bit of wood he said, "I need to put more wood on the fire." Kyle turned toward her slightly so he could get to his feet, and

Cynthia turned her face to him. They kissed. Leaning back on his knees he pulled her up into his arms and covered her face with light soft kisses—all over her eyes, her nose, her forehead, and then his mouth found hers again. With his lips slightly parted he kissed her like Rick never had.

Rick had always stuck his tongue down her throat like he was trying to strangle her. Kyle kissed with his lips, just the tip of his tongue caressing hers so gently yet so very passionately. His kisses left a trail of fire across her cheek as he stopped to nibble her ear then ever so slowly traveled down her neck.

As he gently eased her down on her back, his lips continued their path of burning kisses along her collarbone to the soft spot at the base of her throat. With his left arm behind her neck and his right hand lightly resting on her chest, his fingers tentatively undid the first button of her blouse—then another button, with his lips following as the neckline parted.

Panting in little gasps, thinking only of his lips and the tingling kisses he was tracing ever farther down her chest, Cynthia knew she must stop him. As much as she might want this moment to go on she couldn't. With regret she placed her hand on his chest and gently pushed him up and away. In a breathy voice she said, "No. Please. I can't! Please stop."

Kyle looked into her eyes and whispered, "I want you—but we only just met today. I understand." With great effort he pulled away from her.

She felt the chill of the air on her bare chest, and truly didn't want him to take away the warmth that had been there only a second ago, but she had to stop. She wasn't here for romance but to find a way to save her very life.

He sat up and stared into the dying embers. "I better go."

"Wait, we haven't talked about the museum, and Dr. Smith, and his cures, and ... and ..." As she pulled her blouse together and sat up, there was a look of rejection and hurt on his face.

"If that's all you're interested in, I'll meet you at the museum and open it for you tomorrow. Pick a time."

"Please don't be offended. It's not that I don't want you. You don't understand. I have questions, I have to know things, learn things." He was on his feet and headed for the door. She cried, "Please wait!"

He opened the door and said stonily, "Pick a time. I'll be there."Her head was spinning. Why was he leaving? Was he that touchy? Couldn't he wait at least a little? He was at the open door. He turned and looked at her, his eyes questioning. She stammered, "Nine ... nine thirty?"

"I'll be there." The door banged shut behind him.

FOUR

Kyle stabbed the button on the dashboard harder than necessary. The garage door went up, and lights along the drive, inside the garage, and by the pool came on. As he got out of the car he thought, 'Why did she have to stop us?' Cynthia, with those beautiful eyes, was the first woman his body had responded to in thirty years.'

Poor Brenda! She had tried so hard to understand. She lived with him, slept with him for years, hoping he would want her. He *had* wanted her, loved her, but it was as he had told her—his body might as well be dead for all the physical response a woman could get from it. She even held him when he sat up in bed, screaming in the night from the damned nightmare. They would sit up and drink coffee until he was calm again. Then she would return to bed alone and he would sit, and wait for the sun to come up.

Brenda was the only one he had ever told about the nightmare—or how even when he was awake and trying to make love to a woman, he would see it in his mind: the face, the trembling dying lips, the life slipping from the beautiful eyes of Mei Lin. It was after he told Brenda about it—how he had killed Mei Lin in Viet Nam—that Brenda had finally left him. He didn't blame her. He hoped she had found happiness in California.

Then tonight with Cynthia, his snow angel as he was beginning to think of her, he had felt the stirring down there and then the shocking miracle—an erection, strong and hard as a rock. How could he have explained to her what a tremendous thing she had done for him? Then she had stopped him for no reason he could imagine. He was hurt and angry.

For the ten millionth time he cursed the government and every soul in it for their stupid war. It had taken so many of his friends, and it had even taken his manhood. No one even knew he had been there. Working for the DIA as he had, there were no public records. Everyone thought he had been lucky and never been in the service or Nam. Viet Nam—where he had been when his little sister died in a fiery car crash on the night of her senior prom. Some kind of technical exemption from the draft—yeah, that's what everybody in this small town believed.

He had his nightmare, he had his secret, yet strangely now for the first time in longer then he cared to remember, he had hope. He looked at the kitchen clock. One a.m. It would be a long night until nine, when he could see her again.

FIVE

Cynthia sat on the floor, looking at the dead fire, and cold ashes. Why had he left? Surely other women had asked him to wait? After all it was the first day they'd met! Damn it, she was beginning to get mad. This was not fair! She finished the last of the wine and as she stood, the doorbell rang. She thought, 'He's come back!' and rushed to the door to fling it wide. But there was only the wind and darkness. Standing there, she called, "Hello?" There was only silence, the sound of water dripping from the trees, and the wind—nothing more. She could see that the clouds were parting and the moon was peeking through. It would be full by her birthday, on Halloween, and she would be forty. It might well be her last birthday. She must stop thinking about Kyle, and concentrate on finding the secrets of the museum, the secrets of Dr. Smith. But of course she had her own secret—nobody here knew she was dying.

She thought, 'Too much wine and too much stimulation.' Cynthia locked the door, turned out the lights, and went up to her bedroom. After a hot, then cold shower, she polished her nails and as she sat letting them dry, saw by the bedroom clock it was two in the morning. 'My God! I have to get some sleep if I'm going to be at the museum by nine.'

Sliding under the covers, she drifted off easier than she would have believed. Just as sleep took her, she was remembering Kyle's tender kisses.

SIX

Kyle was wide-awake at six. He hadn't slept much anyway. Damn! He was sorry he had left her last night. But everything happened so fast and his physical reaction to her had made him unsteady as he tried to hold her and slowly make love to her. All those doubts in his mind—would he really be able to complete the act? Would he be able to satisfy her? It had been so very long since he had really made love to a woman, and then she had pushed him away. Why? He knew they'd just met, but it seemed so natural, so wonderful. Had he done something wrong? Maybe she just didn't find him attractive? No, he had spent a lot of time with women, flirting and dating, building a phony reputation as a playboy bachelor. Only the women knew he never took them to bed, but he had learned to read the signs of when they were interested and wanting to sleep with him. Cynthia had definitely shown him she was interested.

So why had she stopped him? The only thing he knew for sure was he wanted to see her again and he would try very, very hard to please her. He could hardly wait for nine o'clock. An idea popped into his head. He would start her day off right. The florist he used in town wouldn't open until ten, but Kyle knew the owner very well. Calling Peggy at home he asked a small favor. Could she deliver a dozen yellow roses to the old Stanton place by eight thirty this morning? For him, she would deliver them personally. What about the card? After a moment's thought he said. "Just sign it Kyle".

Peggy said, "This must be one special lady!"

Kyle replied, "You better believe it. Thanks Peg."

"Any time Kyle. You've been one of my best customers for years, as well as a great friend. Good luck with her."

*   *   *   *

As she hung up, Peggy wondered who could be living in that creepy old Stanton place. Well, she would get a look at this ... what had Kyle said her name was? Oh yeah, Cynthia Dobbs.

*   *   *   *

Cynthia was having her second cup of coffee in the kitchen when the doorbell rang. She thought, 'Not this again.' A glance at her watch told her it was eight thirty. There was only one way to find out. Not expecting anybody to be there, Cynthia jerked open the door and there on her step stood a very pretty redhead, holding a vase of beautiful yellow roses.

The redhead said, "Cynthia Dobbs?" Cynthia nodded. "Hi, I'm Peggy from Town Florists; I have a delivery of roses for you."

"Please come in. Who would be sending me roses? Your shop must open really early to be delivering these at eight thirty a.m."

"We don't open until ten, but the man who sent these is a very good friend of mine and I own the store. His Name is Kyle Dwyer, one of the nicest people you are likely to meet."

Cynthia thought, 'Now I know his last name, and he sent me roses!' To Peggy she said, "If you don't have to go right away, would you like a cup of coffee?"

"I would love one. I had just gotten up when Kyle called and he insisted I get these here by eight thirty. A cup of coffee sounds wonderful."

"Do you give this kind of service to all of your customers? You must have a very successful business if you do. But I would think the effort would kill you." Leading Peggy back into the kitchen and putting the flowers on the table, she got another cup from the cabinet and said. "How do you take it?"

"Cream and two sugars, and no I don't give this kind of service to all my costumers. But Kyle is very special. My husband and he were good friends for years and years. When Tim died three years ago, I was devastated. Kyle helped me get through all of it and I think I would have lost the florist shop if it hadn't been for him. He and Brenda worked to keep the shop open and me in one piece for about six months. Did you just buy this place?"

"No, it belonged to my grandmother. I'm sorry about your husband. Was it sudden and unexpected? It was nice of Kyle, and did you say Brenda to help you."

"I was in shock. Tim went out to deliver an order and next thing I know the hospital is on the phone telling me he had a heart attack. Kyle and Brenda were in the store at the time looking for flower arrangements for the Historical Society to put on veterans' graves on Memorial Day. They drove me to the hospital and were right there with me when I learned Tim had died. It was a good thing they had taken me I don't think I could have driven home by myself. Everything was such a mess and they were so wonderful in helping me. When Brenda left Kyle, it must be almost two years now,' I tried to cheer him up and help him. But he's so strong-willed and he just seemed to get over her leaving. I don't know. Have you known Kyle long? Did you know Brenda?"

"As a matter of fact, I just met him yesterday, and I've never heard of Brenda. I came here to research my family history—find out some things about old Dr. Smith, and Egg Harbor City in general. I lived here until I was nineteen, but I don't seem to know anybody in town anymore. Then my mother and I moved away to Glenfalls, and it's even smaller then Egg Harbor. Oh my, look at the time—it's after nine. I hate to rush you out, but I must get to the museum. Kyle said he would meet me there and open it so I could do research."

"I must be going anyway. I have to stop home before I open the shop for the day. We are only open for four hours on Sunday, but that's from ten to two. Thank you for the coffee, and say hi to Kyle for me. Good luck with your research and with this house. So nice to have met you, stop by the store sometime."

"Thanks I will—nice to have met you too." Closing the door, Cynthia had to hurry to finish getting ready. She changed into black slacks, a bulky knit sweater, and her snow boots. There wasn't any snow on the ground but the ankle high snow boots were fleece lined and waterproof, so her feet would stay warm and dry.

Suddenly she realized it would be too warm in the museum to wear the snow boots the whole time, so she changed her heavy socks for a pair of knee-hi's and put a pair of black skimmers in her shoulder bag. With her cell phone, camera, notes, paper, and everything else, it was getting heavy. Nothing to do about it. She grabbed her purse and noticed it was nine forty-five. She could only hope Kyle was late too, or would wait for her.

SEVEN

As Cynthia was going out the door, her cell phone chirped. She dug in her shoulder bag and located the phone, turned it on and heard Kyle's voice say, "Cynthia? Hello? Can you hear me?"

She smiled and said, "Hi, Kyle. Sorry. I'm running a bit late."

She heard, "Hello? Hello? Cynthia, are you there? Can you hear me?"

Damn cell phones! She must be in a dead area. She said, "Kyle if you hear me I'm on my way. Kyle?"

"There you are. Are you coming? I've been at the museum since about nine. Hello?"

"Yes, I'm on my way."

"Good, I can hear you fine now. I'll wait for you."

"I'm just getting in my car and should be there in five minutes. Thank you, Kyle, for the lovely roses. They were a real surprise, but you shouldn't have. I mean, well thanks … it was nice to meet your friend, Peggy."

"Peg is a real special lady. We have been friends for a long time. I'm glad you liked the roses."

"Yes. Hey, I'm here already. I'll be there in just a moment. Bye!" She hung up, stepped from the car, and noticed the bright sunshine sparkling on the serpentine stream across the street. The stream was right up to the top of its banks this morning. 'Must be so full from all the rain yesterday and last night,' she thought.

At the museum, she tried the door. It was locked. How could that be? She was just talking to Kyle and he had said he was here. She jumped as someone put a hand on her shoulder.

Kyle said, "Sorry, I didn't mean to frighten you."

"Well you did. I thought you would be inside."

"I was. I left the main door locked because we aren't really open. Except for you of course. Come around to the side entrance. How are you this morning? You look quite lovely with the sun in your hair."

"Thank you. I'm good—especially since someone sent me roses to start my day. They are very beautiful. But why did you send them? And why yellow roses?"

"He opened the side door for her to enter, and said, "Yellow roses are for friendship, and I hope we can be friends. I sent them because of last night. I'm sorry I left like I did. I—well—uh—sometime maybe I'll be able to explain what happened, but not right now. Look, I pulled out all the written files we have on Dr. Smith. I have them spread out on the kitchen table in the back room. We'll have more room to work back here, and I made coffee and a pot of tea. Would you like a cup? Why don't you settle yourself and start with this pile, I'll go upstairs where we keep the records and see what I can find in newspaper articles about him. Is there a certain year or time period you're interested in?"

"A cup of coffee would be great. It looks like you've really been busy this morning. This is a huge pile of papers and files. I'm mostly interested in cures he did for people. My great-grandmother, Emma Schnee, was treated by him around 1906, so anything we could find about her and how he treated her, as well as what was wrong with her would be wonderful. She and my great grandfather, Max Schnee, came here in that year just for Dr. Smith to treat her. From what I have found out, he cured her."

"I'm afraid we don't have any of Dr. Smith's patient records. I wish we did, but we believe most of them were destroyed when the city took over the buildings and started to use them for government purposes—offices and such. The old sanatorium building was used as the county detention home for boys. Somewhere along the line all the records got lost or thrown away." Putting a mug of coffee on the table in front of her, he went upstairs.

Cynthia took a sip of the delicious dark liquid. Picking up the top file she opened it to find an advertisement for the health resort. In bold letters it said:

HEALTH RESORT across the top, then there was a picture of the sanatorium building with people bathing in the serpentine stream in the foreground. Below the photo it read Charles Smith, M.D. and below that it said: This water will cure Rheumatism of all kinds, Gout, Lameness from Paralysis, Diseases of Uterus and Bladder, Insomnia, Nervous Prostration, all skin and Chronic Disease in General. Under that in bold letters it said: PREVENTS APOPLEXY. On the very bottom it said: To the present open baths, at the Sanatorium, will be added, a Bath Under Glass and with Steam Heating. TELEPHONE 15-03, EGG HARBOR CITY, N.J., there was no date on the ad. Well it certainly looked like Dr. Smith thought he could cure almost anything.

She became very absorbed in the papers and looking through old picture post-cards from the Health Resort. But no matter where she looked she found nothing about tonics made from the magic cedar waters. Just as she was starting to read about the health resort being incorporated in 1905, Kyle came in with a box of news clippings and said, "It's two in the afternoon. Could I interest you in taking a break, and going somewhere for lunch with me?"

Rubbing her eyes and stretching she said, "I didn't have breakfast, so I'm famished! Lunch sounds great. Where do you suggest we go?"

"The Renault Winery is always good, but they serve brunch on Sundays not lunch and I'm not sure what time it ends. I better call."

"Don't you think we had enough wine last night?"

"Dear lady, I didn't say we should drink. I said eat lunch." He winked at her and picked up the phone.

EIGHT

Ten minutes later they were on their way in Kyle's Porsche. The autumn leaves spun up behind them in the cool air as they drove out to the Renault winery. As they drove into the parking lot Cynthia exclaimed, "It says wine tasting tours."

"Yes, the winery was built in the 1860's. It's almost as old as Egg Harbor is. Maybe we could take the tour after lunch. I think they have them until five o'clock. It's only two thirty, so we will have plenty of time to do that if you want to."

"Want to! I would love to. Do you think we could take the tour first and then instead of lunch we could maybe have an early dinner?"

"I don't see why not, although it might make it a bit late to go back to the museum. Tomorrow is Monday and I have things I have to take care of in the morning, so I won't be able to open the museum for you until mid-afternoon. Do you mind?"

Cynthia needed all the time she could get in the museum, but not wanting to interfere with things Kyle needed to do, she said, "No, that would be fine, but could we spend a little time at the museum after dinner?"

"My lady, your wish is my command." He parked and opened her door to help her out. As she took his hand, she looked up into his eyes—he was smiling. She smiled back and felt a warm thrill all through. He led her over the small covered footbridge, across a tiny stream with ducks and swans swimming in it. The grounds of the winery were like some beautiful German parkland, with grass and giant old oak trees. As they walked he pointed out the entrance to the winery restaurant, and a gazebo in a beer garden.

At the far end of the building they came to a set of big double doors. Kyle held one open for her and she walked into a fairy-land of twinkling lights and hundreds of sparkling wine glasses in display cases. She exclaimed, "Oh, how beautiful!

"This is the wineglass museum. The owners have collected all kinds of strange and wonderful wine glasses from across the world. It looks like a tour is just starting. We better try to join this one. We can look at the glasses and things when we return." They hurried across the front room of the wine glass museum, and joined the tail end of a group tour.

Cynthia was thrilled with the beauty of the interior of the winery. The tour they had joined was about ten people including Kyle and her. The tour guide's voice echoed in the vaulted spaces of the pressing and barrel rooms. Later as they moved into the office area she saw a large portrait painting of Louis Nicholas Renault, and just then the tour guide was saying, "… in the 1920's during prohibition the winery made a medicinal health tonic. It was of course a way to get around the law. You chilled the tonic and you had wine. Like magic!"

The group laughed. Cynthia wondered if the tonic was like the ones Dr. Smith had made from the local cedar waters. But the tour was moving on to the best part of the tour for most of them, the tasting room. "Kyle do you know anything about the Renault tonics?"

"Not really, just what the guide said. We have an old bottle of it on display with the wine industry things at the museum. Why do you ask? They say it was nasty tasting stuff."

"I … well … it just took my interest, that's all. I hope they have a good Renault Merlot."

"Of course they do, Renault does make a wonderful vintage Merlot. Also, they do some other excellent wines. Renault winery is one of the best kept secrets of South Jersey. Just wait until you taste their blueberry champagne!"

A few minutes later Cynthia was in complete agreement with his statement. The wine tasting always started with the blueberry champagne. After several other kinds of wine it ended with a dessert cream sherry. The tour was over and they exited through the wine and gift shop. With a shy smile Cynthia said, "Lets get a bottle of Renault Merlot for later tonight. That is, of course, if you will come to my place for a nightcap when we finish at the museum?"

He returned her smile, and winked. "I think you'll have to buy a corkscrew. They don't make screw top, and it is a bit more expensive. And yes, a nightcap sounds great. However I think we should go to the dining room for dinner now.

It's after four, and you are still hoping to stop back at the museum for a while aren't you?"

"Oh yes, I want to look at some more of those papers and would you show me where the bottle of Renault Tonic is on display? That blueberry champagne would be great for a birthday party or some other celebration."

"I will be happy to show you anything you want to see. Speaking of birthdays, mine was on Easter this year. It happens every so often. When's yours?"

"You are so lucky. Your birthday is on a holiday once in a while. Mine is always on a holiday—Halloween. You wouldn't believe some of the weird things I have gotten as gifts over the years."

"Halloween? That's great. It's my favorite holiday, and it's this week. There is a big costume party at the Sweetwater Casino. They have one every year. Would you like to go?"

"With you, to a costume party? I haven't been to one in years, and I don't have anything to wear. Long ago I had a costume birthday party, some friends surprised me with it, they even had a witch dress and hat for me to put on, it was great fun. I guess I could come up with something."

As they walked up to the maitre d' Kyle said, "Charles, how are you? Good, good, glad to hear it, we need a table for two please?" Charles seated them near a small stained glass window. They couldn't see out but the fading afternoon sunlight made a rainbow of colors as it shone through.

The waiter came with a pitcher of ice water and filled their glasses. Then he handed them each a menu and explained about the prix-fixe dinner style. "Six courses in all," he said, "you select the entrée you would like and each is served with five other superb courses from appetizer to dessert along with two wine samplings. All included in the price of the entrée. If there are no questions, I'll return shortly to take your order."

Cynthia was looking around at the dark wooden walls, a huge fireplace, and antique furniture. "It looks like it's been here forever."

Kyle thought the look on her face was enchanting. "Not quite that long. But the booth we are sitting in was made from an oaken wine cask that is about 100 years old. This room was called the 'Method Champenoise.' It is where they first made Renault's wonderful white Champagne—the same white that is used to make the blueberry champagne you enjoyed so much. They make the white, and then in a secret process they add blueberry juice."

Cynthia opened her menu. "You seem to know everyone. You must come here often. What do you suggest I try? It all looks very tempting."

"It is all very good. I don't get here as often as I would like, but when I do I have the 'Grilled Tornadoes of Beef'. They serve it with a Madeira wine and truffle sauce that is magnificent. Of course you might not want beef. If you would like seafood, lamb, or veal the chef does wonderful things with all of it."

"I think the 'Seafood Provencal'; shrimp, scallops, and lump crab meat in white wine sauce sounds too good to pass up. What will the other courses be?"

"They are different every night. The gourmet chef reworks the menu everyday. The entrees are the same but with a different appetizer, salad, sorbet, etc. so while you might have the same entrée it is still a different meal than you would have eaten here the night before."

"How unique! It's really a beautiful room, and it looks like a band is setting up on the other side of the fireplace. Do they have music every night?"

"Yes, it's a four piece combo and believe it or not the restaurant encourages dancing while you dine. Ah, here's the waiter to take our order. Would you like a drink while we wait for the food?"

"I would. Since I'm having seafood, I'll have a glass of white zinfandel please."

Kyle gave their orders to the waiter, and then looked at Cynthia. "I love this old song they're playing; it's the theme from Love Story. Would you care to dance, while we wait for our drinks?"

Cynthia was glad she had changed from her snow boots to her skimmers at the museum, and had decided not to change back when they left for lunch. But she wished they were heels when Kyle took her in his arms and her head was even with his chest. Then looking up into his smiling face she thought 'I don't care,' and gave him a mischievous wink.

By the time the music ended he was holding her very close and she had her head resting against his chest. She could hear his heart beating. She felt safe and warm in his arms, and thought, 'If only we could just stay this way forever.'

Kyle led her back to their table and held her chair for her. Taking his own seat, he picked up his glass and made a toast. "To the best dancer and most lovely partner it has been my pleasure to dance with in a very long time."

Cynthia smiled and took a sip of her Zinfandel. "Thank you sir. The pleasure was all mine. You are a very good dancer. Do you realize we didn't get back to the wineglass museum after the tour? I so wanted to see at all of it."

"They're open every day. You'll have plenty of time to see it."

Cynthia thought, 'Time is the one thing I don't have plenty of. Should I tell him I have less then a year to live? What would he do? How would he react? I don't know him well enough yet. But it's unfair to let him think we could have something together when I know my time is running out.'

"Penny for your thoughts? You look like you were about a million miles away." "A penny is about all they are worth. Now they're playing 'Misty'; it's is one of my favorites. Will you dance with me again before they bring our food?"
"Of course."
On the dance floor she escaped into the warm safety of his arms once more.

*   *   *   *

Holding her so close, with the scent of her hair, and the feel of her in his arms, Kyle felt his body respond. He thought, 'If only I could tell her what magic she has done for me. What is it about her that makes my body respond like it has for no other in years and years? I want so very much to make love with this woman.'
The music ended and they returned to their table just as their appetizers arrived. Cynthia smiled with pleasure, "Portobello mushroom caps stuffed with crab meat—I love them!" Taking a bite, she closed her eyes in sheer pleasure. "These are fantastic. Do you like them?"
"Oh yes, these are excellent. There are very few things in the way of food that I don't like."
"Really, so what don't you like?"
"Well, ah … okra for one thing. I think it's slimy. But they put it in gumbo in New Orleans and I do like gumbo."
"Have you spent much time in New Orleans?"
"No, but I did live in Texas for a time and I got to visit New Orleans often. It is a fascinating city. Have you been there?"
"Yes, I've traveled quite a lot over the years. New Orleans is great but I think my most memorable trip was to the Mediterranean on a cruise about twelve years ago. It was a wonderful trip but I was taken ill and had to return to the states earlier than I was supposed to."
"That's a shame. I've been very fortunate all the times I have traveled. I was always well—never got sick on a trip—just lucky I guess. Did you miss very much of your cruise?"
"Only about three days. But I was very ill. It was at least a month until I was completely well again. Where else have you been?"
"Quite a lot of places in the U S—Hawaii, California, Alaska, the New England states—Texas of course."
"But not much overseas?"

*   *   *   *

His eyes seemed far away for a second, as if the shadow of a very bad memory passed across his face. It was gone in an instant, and she wasn't sure she had seen any change in his smile at all. He said, "Only merry old England—London. I was there for a few weeks looking into the family history. I didn't find as much as I had hoped to, but I got caught up in sightseeing. It is such a fantastic country. Next thing I knew, my three-week vacation was gone and I haven't been able to get away again. I still hope to go back someday and finish what I started."

"Your family is English?"

"Only on my mother's side. Mostly I'm German. But I don't speak the language and I have never been lucky enough to visit Germany. So, sweet lady, where do your ancestors come from? You did say one of your reasons for coming back to Egg Harbor was family history research"

"I have a little bit of most of Europe in me I think, but more Italian, Scott, and German than anything else. My great-grandfather, Max Schnee, was right from Germany. His mother was Scottish, and his wife, Emma, was Sicilian—about as Italian as one can get."

Just then the waiter came with dessert. "Your fried cheesecake. Would you like coffee with that?"

"Coffee would be good for me. Cynthia, coffee?"

"Yes, please. I have never had, nor even heard of fried cheesecake. It looks delicious and about a million calories!"

"Don't you know about dessert in a good restaurant? They take out the calories in the kitchen and feed them to the chef. That is why all really good chefs are so fat."

They laughed together and Cynthia was once again taken by the deep rich sound of his laughter. His eyes were twinkling and she thought, 'What a wonderful, funny, handsome man he is.'

NINE

Later, on the way back to the museum, with laughter in her voice she said, "I am stuffed! Shame on you Kyle Dwyer, we were just going out for lunch."

"Didn't you enjoy it? We'll still be back at the museum by seven thirty. You should have at least a few hours for research. After all you did learn some things about Egg Harbor City, most certainly about Renault Winery, and don't forget the glass museum you want to go back and see. Of course I admit the meal wasn't anything special. But what can you do?" She looked at him, he looked at her, and they both cackled with glee.

A few minutes later, as Kyle opened the car door for her, she felt the nip in the autumn air. It was a beautiful night with millions of stars overhead. "Isn't it beautiful out here Kyle? The moon will be up in another hour or two. But right now it's so dark, just after sunset and the sky and stars are breathtaking."

"Yes … I have always loved a clear cool autumn night. It's so refreshing after the heat of the summer months. Fall is my favorite time of year. Look! You can see the big dipper just coming up over the trees."

As they stood there and gazed at the sky, Cynthia leaned against his side and felt his arm move gently around her shoulders. She turned in his arms and looked up into his face. He leaned his head slowly toward her and placed a soft tender kiss on her lips. Pulling back, he whispered, "We should go in or you won't have any time for research."

She knew he was right, but oh how much she wanted another of his kisses. She nodded, and they went into the museum. Sitting again at the table in the kitchen she picked up the next file folder. It contained many old photographs of people in the water. One eight by ten showed several women up to their waists. It had a caption at the bottom that read, 'A group of women enjoying the waters in the first leg of the serpentine creek.' It also listed their names. Cynthia's heart began to race as she read the name of a woman in a large hat in the center of the group. Emma Schnee. It was her great-grandmother! "Kyle come look at this—it's my great-grandmother!"

Kyle leaned over her shoulder and stared at the grainy black and white photo. "It's not very clear, but I would definitely say beauty runs in your family."

"I don't know about that but this must have been taken when she was here for treatments in about nineteen-oh-six. I wish I could have a copy of this."

"Dear lady, your wish is my command. We have a photo quality copier here and I can make one for you in about a minute."

"That would be wonderful. Before we forget, could you show me where that bottle of Renault Tonic is on display?"

"Sure, I'll show you while the copier warms up. It's right over here in the case with the wine industry information. In fact I'll take it out so you can have a good look at it." He led her to a glass display case on the other side of the museum. Reaching in from the back he picked up a tall clear glass bottle filled with a murky yellowish liquid and handed it to her.

Holding it up to the light, she could read the faded label. "Renault Tonic—good for what ails you. Warning: Do not refrigerate or product will turn to wine." She grinned. "How strange that they would put a warning label on it."

Kyle chuckled, "You did hear the tour guide say it was a way to get around the prohibition laws. Look, there was a card under the bottle, it must have fallen down and no-one noticed." He handed her the card.

"It says, 'Renault Tonics were 44 proof alcohol with the addition of an ingredient called peptone. When refrigerated, the peptone separated and you had white or red wine, depending on the tonic you bought.' Who do you think wrote this card?"

"One of our members I'm sure. Maybe Margie or Adele; they are in charge of the displays and are some of our founding members. But it could be anyone of the volunteers here at the museum. One of them found the information and typed up the card. The copier is ready. I'll make the copy of the picture you wanted."

He walked to the other side of the museum and Cynthia was left standing with the old bottle of Renault Tonic in her hands thinking, 'Could the cure for me be something like this, something so very simple? This of course was just a way to get around the law. But did Dr. Smith make something similar from the cedar water that really cured people?'

"Earth to Cynthia, Earth to Cynthia."

She realized Kyle was standing next to her, smiling and trying to hand her the photo.

"I'm sorry. I was about a million miles away just then. The museum is very interesting. You have lots of wonderful things here." She took the picture from his hand, "Is this the copy?"

"Yes, I adjusted the contrast a little and it's much clearer, don't you think?"

"This is wonderful! You can really see her face clearly now. Thank you Kyle."

"Glad to do it. Pictures are so very important in family history research. Sometimes they can tell us so much more then a written description. Look—you can see the round stepping-stones that made up the path along the water. Over in Peace Pilgrim Park you can find bits of the path leading away from the remaining foundation stones of the sanatorium."

"Really? Where do they lead?"

"Not anywhere anymore. It seems Dr. Smith was very fond of paths made of stepping-stones. You find short pieces of them all around the area. I think maybe we better be going if we are going to have that nightcap you mentioned."

Cynthia looked at her watch. "It's almost ten! Where does the time go? Should we put all the files and things away, or can we leave them until we come back. Speaking of which, when can you be here to let me in again?"

TEN

They locked up the museum and headed for the old Stanton place. As she pulled into the driveway, Cynthia saw a skinny white cat run across the lawn. She thought, 'Poor kitty—must be a stray.'

Kyle parked behind her and hurried to open her car door. As she stepped out she said, "Thank you sir. Did you see that poor cat?"

"No, why do you say poor cat?"

"It was so skinny, with long hair, but it looked matted."

"Probably just a stray. Do you like cats?"

"Yes, but I don't have any. There is this one big old cat, 'Bootsie,' that belongs to the neighbor at my mother's old house. He gets in all the time—I don't know how. But he comes to visit, if you know what I mean."

"He comes to beg for food?"

"No, not really. I don't feed him much, a bit of milk or a little tuna juice if I've made a sandwich. Mostly he just wants to be picked up and loved."

"By you? A very smart cat; I would say he has excellent taste in women." Kyle gave her a big wink and a smile that made her feel warm all over.

Cynthia grabbed the bottle of merlot from the car and led the way to the porch. As she unlocked the front door, Kyle reached around and pushed the door open for her. His face was next to her ear and she could feel his warm breath on her cheek. The scent of his aftershave made her a little dizzy with anticipation. Stepping inside and heading for the kitchen she said, "I'll get the glasses; it's chilly and damp in here, why don't you light a fire in the hearth?"

"Kind of difficult with only two pieces of wood. Do you know if there's any more around?"

"I think there is a small stack outside by the side door here in the kitchen. Take the flashlight. I must get those outside lights fixed. They probably just need new bulbs."

"If you have any, I could install them in a minute." He opened the kitchen door and shined the light around. The outside light fixture was right there next to the door; he could see the glass globe was missing and the light bulb was broken.

"Yes, there are some in this top cabinet." He came back in as she was trying to reach the bulbs. Standing behind her, he reached above her to get one. As he reached up his body pressed against her, trapping her between him and the counter. She could feel the warmth of him and she could tell he was aroused. It was only for a moment, and then he had stepped away from her. She turned around and he was just standing there with the light bulb in his hand and a curious look on his face. She thought, 'he wants to kiss me! Why doesn't he kiss me? Damn!'

But in the next moment he turned and walked to the door saying, "It's only a sixty watt bulb, so it won't be very bright for outside, but if it works it's better then nothing." He thought, 'Just being near her and my body reacts like I'm a teenager again. I must go very slowly and not frighten her again like last night.'

A few minutes later he reached in the door and flicked the switch. "You were right; all it needed was a bulb. I see there is some firewood, stacked right here; we'll have a fire in two shakes. How is that wine coming?"

Twisting the corkscrew into the bottle she was thinking, 'The wine is almost ready and so are you. Why didn't you kiss me?' She said, "It will be ready when you are. I will take it in by the fireplace."

When he came in, carrying an armload of wood, she was sitting by the hearth on the faded carpet where they had been last night. He thought, 'She is so beautiful, to hell with the fire, I want to take her right now and feel her in my arms, cover her with kisses, drink in the scent of her hair, and oh, God how I want to kiss those lips.'

She said, "Will that be enough?"

He chuckled deep in his chest.

She asked, "What's so funny?"

"Just a stray thought about how beautiful you are. I have to go out and find some kindling, think you could rustle up some old newspaper while I'm out there?"

"Of course. Don't be too long." She got the newspaper than sat waiting for him to return. Looking at the beautiful dark red wine in her glass she thought, 'I know he's interested. I hope he isn't still put off about last night. But he did send me the roses and said he was sorry about leaving so abruptly. I want him to hold me tight like he did when we were dancing. I felt so warm and safe against his chest, in the circle of his arms.'

He came back into the room. "If you stare at that wine glass any harder I fear you will shatter it. I found a covered box of kindling around the back of the house. Do you have a glass for me?"

"Yes, but you promised me a fire in two shakes, yet the hearth is still cold and dark." She pouted.

He thought her mouth was even sexier like that.

"I'll have it going strong in a minute my dear." He took the newspapers from her hand, knelt by the fireplace and sure enough it wasn't even a minute until bright, merry yellow flames were dancing.

She held a glass of wine out to him. "While I was waiting I tried a little sip. You are right, Renault merlot is so much better then screw top." She burst out in a fit of giggles.

He took the glass and sat down beside her and with a smile, poked a finger in her ribs. This resulted in a renewed bout of giggling and the stammered words, "Stop, stop—I'm too ticklish! Ooh."

Laughing, he continued to tickle her, moving his fingers from one side to the other and back, each time gently dragging his hand across her stomach. Slowly his hand found its way under the edge of her sweater to the soft warm skin beneath. Wrestling around together, they almost spilled their wine.

He sat back and took a swallow of the merlot. Setting his glass aside, his hand still under the edge of her sweater, he leaned forward to crush her lips under his. She didn't resist, meeting the fire of his kiss with fire of her own. His hand slid around her back, pulling her into a firm embrace. As he brushed the tip of her nose with his, he slowly trailed a line of burning kisses to her ear. He cradled her in his arms and lay down with her, his fingers worked at the clasp of her bra.

The doorbell rang.

He pulled back, and sat up looking at her, "Did you order pizza again?"

"No! I'm still full from dinner at the restaurant. It's probably nobody. I wanted to tell you about the doorbell before, but it slipped my mind. It rings at the strangest times for no reason that I can see. Like last night when I was waiting for you it rang several times. That's why I was standing at the door when you arrived."

He went to the door and opened it. Darkness and moonlight greeted him. "You say it just rings like that for no reason?" She nodded. "Well, I did tell you this place was supposed to be haunted." He smiled; she looked a little frightened. "Don't be afraid, it's most likely a short in the wiring. If you like I can come by tomorrow afternoon before we go to the museum and take a look at it."

"Are you an electrician too?"

He laughed, "I do a little bit of everything. And now, my dear, I think it's time I was heading home."

"You're kidding right? We were just ... I mean, why must you leave? At least stay and finish your wine."

What Kyle thought was, 'I must go because I want you so and I don't trust myself, and I'm not sure I could complete the act anyway.' What he said was, "It's after midnight and I have early morning business meetings and things. I have papers to prepare before I attend them. Please understand, I really have no choice, I must go."

Cynthia stood up with their wine glasses, and walked over to stand in front of him. She handed him his glass. "If you must go, you must." Staring up at him with anger in her eyes, she finished her wine in a single gulp.

He set his wineglass on the table by the door and took her in his arms and kissed her goodnight. With his tender but passionless, cool kiss she was sure the evening was over. 'But why, why is he leaving again?' she asked herself. 'I didn't push him away this time.' "Kyle, don't go, what's wrong?"

"Nothing's wrong. I have early meetings and it's late; I have to be up early and ..." words failed him. "Good night." He turned and stepped out the door.

She stood in the moonlight and watched him get into his car and drive away, all the while thinking, 'Don't leave me.' His car disappeared down the street.

ELEVEN

She looked up at the moon; it was a beautiful night. Then she heard a soft and tiny squeaky little meow. There at her feet was the skinny white cat, looking pitiful. Cynthia's heart melted. "Would you like to come in and have some milk?" Big blue eyes looked up at her as if to say 'please?' She stepped back and held the door open. The cat walked in with the regal grace of a queen and right on into the kitchen like it knew where it was going.

Cynthia closed the door and hurried after the cat. As she was pouring some Half & Half into a saucer, the cat stroked itself between her ankles and rubbed its head on her feet.

"Good kitty." She scratched the cat behind the ears as she bent down to put the saucer on the floor. The cat went at the bit of milk like it hadn't eaten in days. "Maybe I should see if I have a little meat or something I can give you." Looking in the refrigerator she found the lunch meat she had gotten the night before. "How about some pieces of ham?" The cat looked up at her like it understood what she said.

Cynthia put torn up pieces of ham on the saucer where the milk had been. The cat began munching that. She placed a bowl of water on the floor and sat down to watch the cat eat. Well she thought 'Kyle has left, at least the cat will give me a little company.'

"So kitty, what shall I call you? I don't even know if you're a boy or a girl." The cat had finished the ham and was washing its front paw the way cats do. She picked the cat up and said, "You're so light—nothing like Bootsie, the fat pig. Now let's see." She held the cat up under the front legs at the shoulders and exclaimed, "Oh my, you're a big boy kitty, aren't you?" She giggled a little and cradled the cat in her arms, looking down at his face. "Good kitty," she cooed as she nuzzled her face in the cat's face. The kitty's little pink tongue darted out and licked her nose. Cynthia smiled. "A little kitty kiss, aren't you a sweet guy? You know your hair is all matted, and full of knots. If I'm going to keep you I'll have to find a vet to look you over and a place to have your hair done. I guess with you I should say groomed." The cat began to purr and settled itself in her arms.

"But now my fine feline friend, you must go out and I must go to bed." She carried the cat to the door, when she opened it and tried to put the cat down she felt his claws dig lightly into her arm. "Well I guess you don't like that idea. But I can't let you stay in; I have no litter box for you."

The cat jumped down from her arms and began to nose at the back door. "What are you doing kitty?" Looking at the door Cynthia saw there was a pet door there and it had a hook latch. She clicked the latch open and the cat jumped in and out several times as if to show her he knew what it was for. "Well I'll be. How did you know that was there?" The cat regarded her with a curious stare. "I guess you have your own secrets don't you kitty. I suppose you can stay in with me. But no messes or out you go."

Cynthia locked the back door and the cat followed her up to the bedroom. She pulled on her old lacy cotton nightshirt—the one Rick called a poet's shirt—and slipped between the covers. She was very tired and a little angry with Kyle. What a strange man he was getting to be, but he did have wonderful kisses. She was just dozing off when the bed shook. Startled, Cynthia sat up and clicked on the bedside lamp. The cat had jumped up on the bed to join her. "Look mister cat if you are going to sleep with me you need to get up on the bed before I'm dropping off to sleep." The cat settled himself between her feet and looked up at her as if to say, "Well, turn out the light." She did and shortly they were both sound asleep.

TWELVE

Kyle drove the Porsche to a winding back road in the Wharton State Forest that had sharp curves and some long straight stretches. With the windows down and the wind whipping in at a hundred miles an hour on the straight-aways, he found himself thinking of Cynthia. 'Why with the first woman my body has reacted to, did everything have to be such a mess? All those other women so willing to be with me, and nothing happened—nothing worked. Now I find one that gets me going and makes me feel like a normal man and what happens? Always something! Her or me ... and what the hell was with that damn doorbell tonight?' Banging his hand on the steering wheel, he smashed his foot ever harder on the gas pedal.

Kyle knew these back roads like the lines of his hand. In high school he and his friends used to come out here late at night to search for the Jersey Devil. He knew the bends in the roads and where all the old abandoned "haunted" houses were, all the way out to Leeds Point. There you could still find the foundation stones of the old Leeds house where the Jersey Devil was supposedly born. He also knew from Viet Nam that there were far worse things in this world than ghosts and devils.

He arrived home at about three in the morning and worked on the papers he would need for the meeting with his accountant and lawyer in the morning. At last he lay down in bed about five a.m. He slept until Mei Lin entered his dreams. Her smiling face—so real—as real as her blood pouring over his hands, turned his dream into a nightmare. He sat up screaming. It was seven in the morning.

THIRTEEN

Cynthia suddenly woke at seven am. She felt a chill like a cold hand had touched her cheek. The sun was streaming in the bedroom window and the cat was sitting on the windowsill watching some early morning birds flit by.

Her first thought was of Kyle. He would be busy this morning and so should she. Getting up, she scratched the cat's head. "Good morning kitty, lots of birds out there? It looks like a beautiful day. As soon as I get washed and dressed I'll see about some breakfast for us."

In the kitchen she made coffee and scrambled eggs with pieces of ham that she shared with the cat for his breakfast. "While I'm out today I'll get you some proper cat food and a comb and brush. Kyle didn't say what time he would come by today so I'll be back not later than one o'clock. What do you think? Is that early enough? Of course if it's too early you and I may have a long wait, kitty."

After doing the dishes she went upstairs and dressed in blue jeans, sturdy loafer walking shoes and a red cotton shirt. Red always looked so good with her dark hair. As she came downstairs she saw the cat lying on one of the living room chairs. "Be good kitty—mommy will be back in a few hours."

As she was driving through downtown she saw Peggy just opening the front door of Town Florists. On impulse, Cynthia pulled into the curb and parked next to Peggy's car. "Hi Peg! Just opening for the day?"

"Hi Cynthia. Yes, if you want to keep in business you need to be here when the customers want you to be. Come on in and see the shop. If you have time I'll have a pot of coffee going in two shakes. Would you like a cup? Come inside." She opened the door and led the way.

"I'd love to see your shop and I can certainly handle one more cup of coffee. It's a beautiful day isn't it? I love fall. Oh, your shop is lovely and decorated for Halloween too!"

"I love fall too," said her new friend. "I do a bit of decorating for most holidays. It tends to help with sales. Puts the customers in the mood to buy I guess. How did your research go at the museum? Was Kyle helpful? I can't imagine him not being, he knows a lot about this town."

"He was a big help, and I found out some interesting things. We had dinner at the Renault Winery last night. We took the tour and I want to visit the wineglass museum today. There just wasn't enough time yesterday. It's a beautiful place. As a matter of fact, I was on my way there just now, when I saw you opening the shop."

Peggy led her to the back room and started the coffee maker. "Yah, it's a great place—almost as old as Egg Harbor City itself. They have beautiful grounds and some really great old oak trees. After Tim died, I spent a lot of time walking the grounds for peace and solitude. Well, there and out at the lake. Have you been to the lake?"

"Not since I got back, but when we used to live here my mom and I would go out there on picnics, swimming in the summertime and ice skating in the winter. I even used to ride my bike out there in the fall after school to enjoy the cool air and look at the beauty of the autumn colors. The leaves were so magnificent!"

"We're not New England, but we do get some great fall colors most years. This one has been really good. I guess it has to do with how fast we get a cold snap to turn the leaves. Tim always says ... I mean said 'it takes one really cold night early in October to make a good color show for the fall.' We ... we used to love to take long walks through the fallen leaves and feel the first real nip in the air. Then we'd go home and have a fire with a glass of wine. I loved him so much and I miss him so very badly." Her eyes were moist, and emotion stopped her words.

Just then the door buzzer sounded as a customer entered the shop. Peg walked out to the front of the store and said. "Carol, how are you this fine morning? Come to pick up the arrangement you ordered yesterday?"

"Yes, and it's a really beautiful day out there. I was going to come by later but when I saw the bright blue sky and felt the nip in the air, I couldn't wait another minute to be out of the house."

"Carol this is Cynthia, she just moved back to town. She's staying in the old Stanton place. You know, over by the railroad on Atlantic Avenue? We were just about to have a cup of coffee. Would you like to join us?"

"Pleased to meet you," Carol said, nodding at Cynthia. "Aren't you afraid staying in that haunted house? It gives me the creeps just thinking about it. I've always been scared to death of ghosts. Sorry, Peg but I can't stay for coffee. If you could just let me get my flowers, I'll be on my way. Lots to do you know."

After Carol left, Peggy said, "She is such a flit. She's married to a doctor and has more time and money than she knows what to do with but she's also afraid of everything—even her own shadow. Now don't get me wrong; she is a good person. That arrangement she just picked up is for her family plot out at the cemetery. She changes them with the seasons. Of course they don't last very long because the caretakers remove them."

"Is it really supposed to be haunted?"

"What?"

"My house, the old Stanton place as everybody calls it. This isn't the first time I've heard that it is dangerous or full of ghosts or something. I don't recall any talk like that when Mom and I lived here with my grandmother."

"Well … there are rumors that the old lady who lived there was a witch. I guess that would have been your grandmother. They say that the night she died there was such a storm that it shook the whole town with bolt after bolt of lightning. People are superstitious and word is that the storm was because a really bad witch's soul was on its way to hell."

"I don't believe a word of it," Cynthia replied somewhat indignantly. "My grandmother was one of the sweetest people that ever lived. How could anybody think she was a witch? Mom and I lived there with her for nine years after my dad died, until we moved to Glenfalls. Ghosts and witches? Phooey! Who would have started such a rumor?"

"I don't know. It's always been talked about that way. I always thought it was just one of those old stories people tell to frighten little children. You know, every old town has to have its secrets and its ghosts."

"I suppose, but it's different when it's your house and your grandmother they are talking about. Mom and I never heard a word about such a thing before we moved away. No one said we lived in a haunted house or that Gran was a witch. She only lived about five years after we moved. Mom should have come here and cleaned it out and sold it long ago but there was always something more pressing. I guess I'm fortunate she kept the taxes paid on it, or I would be living in a motel. Look, I really must be going. Thanks for the coffee, and you really do have a lovely shop. I'll come by another time and visit some more, if that's okay?"

"Sure stop by anytime. Ten to six Monday through Saturday, and ten to two on Sunday. This store is my life. Can you tell?" She gave Cynthia a sad smile.

On impulse Cynthia hugged her. "I'll see you again soon I promise." As she walked out to her car Cynthia thought, 'How sad that Peg lost her Tim, it's so obvious she loves him still.'

When she arrived at the Renault winery, she was struck again by the beauty of its grounds and buildings. Crossing over the tiny stream she bought some dry corn kernels from a vending machine and fed the big ducks and geese that waddled along the stream bank. 'What an idyllic setting,' she thought. 'No wonder it's so popular for weddings.' She strolled slowly toward the entrance to the wineglass museum.

FOURTEEN

Kyle's accountant, Nino, said, "Kyle, I don't know why you want to do this. Putting all of your assets in a revocable trust for the Historical Society is a noble idea, but you're not that old. Shit man, forty-nine is young these days. Old people put their things in trust for their grandkids and such when they're getting ready to die or go into a nursing home or some such thing. You're young and healthy, or is there something you're not telling me? Besides, if you want the historical society to have your money just leave it to them in your will."

Kyle's lawyer, David, said, "He's already done that."

"Then what's with this revocable trust stuff?"

"Gentleman, please! I got you two here today to advise me about this trust I want to set up. I want it set up now, and I want it because I don't want the money to just get spent on whatever they might spend it on after I'm gone. I want it to last to take care of the museum forever. If we get this thing set up properly it will produce income sufficiently large enough each year to take care of the museum's needs. And Nino, there isn't anything you don't know about, but anyone can drop dead anytime. So I want the money to be handled in the right way to make it last. Set it up so in the event of my death the house and other real estate holdings will be liquidated and the proceeds put into the investment portfolio to produce the income necessary for whatever needs the museum may have each year and so the balance will grow by ten percent or more every year. Do it gentleman; it's what I pay you for. I want it revocable so in the event I change my mind, we can undo this again."

David said, "The trust is fairly easy; the forms are standard, but you make me uneasy Kyle. I don't understand why you're doing this now. If you were at least in your sixties it would be different. You don't even have a wife and kids yet. You could you know, one day, and that would change your needs a lot."

"Yes, David it would. That's why I want it revocable. I told you that. Now when can you have the papers ready for me to sign?"

"Well, I'll need some numbers from Nino, but I don't see why we can't have this ready by next Thursday. What's the rush, Kyle?"

"I have other things I want to do; my oil stock is way up right now. I'm going to use that for the initial funding of the trust. Unless there is something else, I think we are finished here. David, just call me when the papers are ready. Nino thank you for coming and you will get those numbers to David won't you?"

"I will, but I still don't like it."

Kyle thought, 'if you knew what I'm planning to do you'd like it a whole lot less, my friend.' He said, "You don't have to like it, Nino, just do it. I know I can depend on you."

After his lawyer and accountant had left, Kyle sat in his study thinking about the decision he had made. Suicide was such a nasty word.

FIFTEEN

Cynthia had spent much more time in the wineglass museum than she had intended. But oh, the things on display were breathtaking! The glassmaker's art was displayed in every color of the rainbow and all the shapes the imagination of man could conceive. It was fantastic.

She was staring at a pair of very tall champagne flutes, thinking 'How wonderful it would be to sip Renault's blueberry champagne from them with Kyle holding me.' Her reverie was shattered when a hand on her shoulder made her jump. Turning quickly she was face to face with Carol, the lady who was so afraid of ghosts. "Oh, you startled me."

"I'm sorry. I am here at Renault's planning a big luncheon for the Republican Ladies Club, and I saw you through the doorway. They have some lovely things here don't you think? Of course this building has its ghosts too. But nothing like that dreadful house where you are staying. Tell me, have you seen or heard anything unusual in that place? I can't imagine where you find the courage to stay there. It must be terrible!"

"Not really, I grew up in that house. I must tell you, I don't know where anyone would get the idea that it is haunted. My grandmother lived there all her life and she was such a sweet person."

"Your grandmother? Mrs. Stanton? The witch? Your grandmother was the witch? Oh my God! Now you are here—are you a witch too? Do you carry her tainted blood?" She put the back of her hand to her mouth, her eyes filled with fear. Carol, the wealthy doctor's wife, almost ran from the room as she quickly retreated.

Cynthia, left standing alone, watched her go and thought, 'What a strange person—it must be terrible to live in such fear. I almost feel sorry for her, but she said some nasty things about my family. To hell with her! I won't let her ruin my day!'

As she left Renault's Cynthia felt the need for some fresh air and decided to drive around the old town and back roads for a while. North on Bremen Avenue, she drove to Indian Cabin Road—an unpaved one lane track through the Pine Barrens—to the Egg Harbor City Lake. Its crystal blue waters sparkled in the October sunshine like a friendly greeting to an old friend. Cynthia parked her car and walked in the light breeze along the lake. The only sound was the wind in the tops of pine trees. So beautiful, so peaceful! She stood near the spillway of the dam and felt the tension leave her. She had always loved the quiet solitude of the lake. Cynthia closed her eyes and took a deep breath, and allowed herself to be at peace.

Kyle's voice broke the stillness. "Not thinking of jumping, I hope?"

She turned, eyes wide. He was standing just a few feet away. The sunlight sparkled in his silver blond hair and a whimsical smile was on his handsome face. "What are you doing here?" she asked. "I thought you had important business meetings today?"

"I did. But it's three thirty in the afternoon now, the meetings are done, so I went by your house to see about the doorbell and nobody was home. I was going to drive to the river and check on my boat when I spotted your car parked here. Am I intruding? Would you like me to go?"

"No, no, I was just enjoying the day. It's so quiet and peaceful here. Isn't it beautiful?"

Kyle looked straight into her eyes. "Yes," he agreed, "very beautiful. If you haven't had lunch, how about I go get a blanket; sandwiches, and some iced tea? We'll have a picnic. Take me about ten minutes."

"Either you're superman or a magician. Ten minutes would be really fast."

"Neither. I live just over there, less then half a mile from the lake. I could nip home, and grab a blanket and things before you know it. Or … you could come with me and we could have lunch at my house."

"I am hungry, sir, and I would like to see your house. So lunch at your place will do nicely. Lead the way."

When she pulled into the driveway of Kyle's house Cynthia was impressed. 'He must have some serious money,' she thought. Before she could get out of her car, Kyle was there opening her door for her and offering a hand to assist. "Such an old fashioned gentleman," she said with a smile, "my mother would love you."

"It's not your mother I'm fond of."

"You're fond of me ... how sweet. Your home is beautiful."

"Thank you. Come on in. We'll rustle up something in the kitchen."

"You have a pool!"

"Yes, I had it put in a few years ago ... I had a friend who loved to swim."

"A friend? What, you don't swim? Must have been some friend to put a pool in for ... her or him?"

"Her. She was a very good friend. She lived here at the time, and I swim like a fish, as they say. What would you like to have for lunch? I have lots of things frozen, we can nuke up a thaw on almost anything."

"Brenda?"

"You want to thaw Brenda? No, yes Brenda ... she was the friend. How do you know about her?"

"Peggy mentioned her. I'm sorry—it's none of my business really, it—just sort of slipped out." 'There I go putting my foot on my mouth again,' she thought.

"No, it's okay. Brenda and I were together for several years—she was a good friend and she helped me through some bad patches, emotionally I mean. Look, how about bacon, lettuce, and tomato sandwiches with iced tea? Would you like a drink first? I make a mean martini, or coffee or ...

"Coffee sounds great. Can we eat out by the pool? I love BLT's and I haven't had one in, I don't remember when. With Jersey tomatoes—I had forgotten about how good they are."

"Sorry, no more Jersey tomatoes. You would have had to be here in July to get them. But you are so right there is no tomato like a Jersey. Something in the soil they say makes them taste so good."

He had been busy in the kitchen while they talked and the bacon was sizzling as he cut up tomatoes and ripped apart lettuce.

"If you show me where the plates and things are, I'll set that little table out by the pool. The sun has moved far enough so it's in the shade. You must show me the rest of your house when we're finished with lunch."

He put plates, napkins, silverware, glasses and a pitcher of iced tea on a tray and handed it to her. As she took the tray, her hands brushed his, and it was like an electric spark between them. She turned and hurried toward the pool as he turned back to his preparations. Each of them had a slightly pleased smile on their face.

She returned through the patio doors that faced the pool and said, "All set. How comes it with the food?"

He turned and handed her a mug of coffee. "Ready in two minutes; why don't you take your coffee and mine out there and I'll be right behind you with lunch." He leaned close and gave her a peck on the cheek. As she carried their coffee mugs out to the table by the pool, Cynthia realized that her cheek was tingling from his small kiss. She smiled.

After lunch they sat by the pool and enjoyed the cool autumn air. The wind rustled the trees and leaves of red and gold floated down around them. "You must love living here; it is so quiet and peaceful. Almost like out at the lake. When I was a girl I spent many fall afternoons there when school let out, with the stillness of the pines and the forest all around. The leaves would rustle and blow in the wind as it rippled the surface water, turning it from light blue to indigo. I think the only time it's more quiet and peaceful is when it's snowing."

"Do you like the snow?" he asked.

"Oh yes! I love the quiet solitude and softness of it as it falls. I don't mean a blizzard with strong winds or anything. But the gentle fall of big flakes late in the afternoon as the day fades to night."

"I know just what you mean. The quiet of it—when the snow is deep and falling straight down—like the world is wrapped in a white woolen blanket. Come to think of it, it's one of the few times I have enjoyed a truly deep and dreamless sleep. Do you ski?"

"I haven't in a while. But I liked it when I had the chance. Are you a ski person? You look like you would be."

"I go whenever I can. The Pocono's aren't that far away, and they have some fair ski resorts, but I really like skiing in Vermont. Unfortunately that is quite a trip from here, eight or ten hours by car." He glanced at his watch. "It's nearly five. If you want to get in any research at the museum, we better be going."

She agreed, and gathered their plates and cups. They carried everything into the kitchen in one trip. Kyle rinsed the dishes and loaded them into the dishwasher while Cynthia looked around at the photos he had on the walls. One was of a very beautiful young woman.

Kyle noticed her interest in that photo and said, "That was my kid sister, I still miss her sometimes. That about does it for the dishes. Shall we go?"

As they were pulling out of the driveway, a red sports car flew by at a high rate of speed, causing Kyle, who was in the lead, to jam on his brakes. Kyle shook his fist out the window at the driver of the sports car. When they arrived at the museum, and Kyle opened her door, Cynthia could see he was still upset. "What's wrong Kyle?"

"That idiot, Sean McCarthy. He drives like a maniac! That was him in the red Mustang sports job that almost hit the front of my car when we were coming out of the driveway."

"You know him? I saw you shake your fist at the car."

"Yah, I know him fairly well. We used to race long ago. I outgrew that, but he never has. I've had a few heated talks with him about driving like that near town. It doesn't matter." He dismissed it with the shake of a hand. Shall we go in? It looks like someone is here."

He opened the side door and followed her into the museum. A slightly bent older man was just coming down the stairs from the library on the second floor. He looked at them and said. "Kyle somebody has made a real mess of the upstairs, and left a pile of papers on the table in the kitchen."

"It's okay Roy it was us. We were just coming back to continue. This is Cynthia Dobbs, Cynthia this is Roy Weiler, one of the members of the society."

Taking her hand, Roy said, "Pleased to make your acquaintance. Miss Dobbs was it? Used to be a Dobbs hereabouts some years ago. Don't know what happened to them. Moved away I expect."

"Yes, it's Dobbs. My mother was Victoria Dobbs. Her maiden name was Stanton and my father was Carl Dobbs. He died when I was ten. I'm trying to find out some things about my family history and Dr. Smith and his magical cures. Do you know much about Dr. Smith's treatments or tonics?"

"Only what's here in the museum. Of course if you want to know about old time Egg Harbor City and the people that lived here you should talk to my Aunt Marie. She was born in 1907, and her mind is still sharp as can be. She could probably tell you some stories about Dr. Smith. She might even have known him. He died in '23 you know. She would have been about sixteen or so at that time."

"Do you really think she might know about his cures and things? Would it be possible for me to meet her? Does she live here in town?"

"Yes, yes and no. She lives in Absecon—that's about eight miles east of here. If you would like, I could call her and see if she would feel up to having some visitors. Of course it's getting kind of late."

"Perhaps you could call her and see if maybe tomorrow or the next day we could visit her?"

"I'll call her and see. She and Jean and Frank—that's her daughter and son-in-law—are most likely having dinner about now. But I know Aunt Marie loves visitors and talking about the past. She's the one that did most of our family history research and put it in nice order—almost like a book."

Kyle said, "Why don't you call her, Roy? Cynthia can continue with her research and I'll clean up the library."

"I'll call her now," he said as he headed to the kitchen where the phone was located.

Cynthia followed and sat at the table and began looking through the pile of folders. In a few minutes Roy said to her, "Would tomorrow afternoon be okay?"

"Oh yes, I'll be glad to go anytime it's convenient for your aunt."

Into the phone he said, "About two? Okay sounds good, we'll see you then." He hung up and turned again to Cynthia. "Two tomorrow afternoon will work for them, and I suppose we could meet here at the museum maybe one-thirty then drive to Absecon."

"It's really not necessary for you to put yourself out. If you tell me how to get there I'm sure I can find it."

"No trouble at all my dear. Besides I haven't been to see Aunt Marie in a week or so. I do like to see her as often as I can, with her being up there like she is— you never know when it will be the last time."

"It isn't necessary for someone to be old for that to be true. Any of us can die at any time.

It seems as if when it's the last time you see them, you don't know it's the last time until later."

"My, my, you sound like me. I'm usually the fatalist in any conversation. Now I must be going. I was just coming downstairs to lock up and leave when you and Kyle arrived. My friend, Margaret, will have supper on the table. We eat together every Monday evening. A pleasure to have met you Miss Dobbs and I'll see you tomorrow afternoon at one-thirty." He called up the steps as he was leaving, "See you later Kyle, and don't forget to lock up when you leave."

"Take care Roy, see you soon." By the time Kyle got to the bottom of the steps, Roy was gone. Standing in the kitchen door he said, "That Roy is a really strange duck. He's good for the society and he works hard in the museum but ... well he is just strange."

Cynthia turned to look at him and they both started to laugh. "He made arrangements for me to meet his aunt tomorrow. He seems kind of sweet in his way."

"His Aunt Marie—now there is a sweet person. Nicest lady you will ever meet. What time did you say we were going down there?"

"I didn't, and I didn't know you were going along."

"Oh yah, I wouldn't miss a chance to see Marie. It's been some time since I've had the pleasure. Besides they will most likely invite us to have tea and cake. That

Jean, Marie's daughter, makes the best pastries around. You will think she's a professional chef when you taste some of her things."

"Kyle, look at this news article. 'Dr. Smith's Fountain of Youth' it says 'Dr. Smith claimed to have been born in 1776, and his longevity came from weekly immersions in the magical cedar water which he discovered in 1859. That year he accidentally fell into nearby Union Creek and emerged wet but cured of all his aches, pains, and ailments. After much experimenting and studying he developed his cedar water cures and opened his health resort in 1897.' It goes on to say. 'Thousands came as weak cripples and left the institution strong and healthy, according to an ad in the 1855–1905 Egg Harbor City Golden Jubilee Souvenir Book celebrating the municipality's first fifty years.' Is there a copy of this golden jubilee book here?"

"Yes, I believe we have a copy. Let me see if I can find it for you." Kyle returned shortly with the book. "Doesn't look a hundred years old does it?"

"No it looks almost new." She took the thin book from Kyle's hands and was soon engrossed, reading it for several hours. When Kyle touched her cheek, she jerked her head up, startled.

"Sorry, didn't mean to frighten you, but I said your name twice with no response."

"It's okay; I was totally absorbed in the history of Egg Harbor. I found the ad for Dr. Smith's Health Resort. It didn't have any more than the news article I saw before." She leaned her head back and put her hand to her mouth to stifle a yawn. "Sorry."

"It is getting late. Did you see the bathing outfit we have on display? It is an original Dr. Smith Health Resort bathing suit."

"No, where?" Kyle led the way to the front of the museum. There, right next to the big glass display case of Dr. Smith's things, was a rack with a single garment hanging on it. Made of heavy black wool, it would cover a person from neck to toe. "Look!" Cynthia exclaimed when she saw the pair of canvas bathing shoes to go with it. "You would think people would be weighted down and drown with all this on."

As she was straightening up from looking at the bathing shoes her eye fell again on the big doctor's book in the glass case that she had seen on her first visit to the museum. 'I want to look in that book!' she thought. But smiling, she turned to Kyle and said, "Can you imagine swimming in that thing?"

"No. But do you swim?"

"Oh, yes! I told you mom and I used to go to the lake in the summers when I was a girl. I think I learned to swim almost before I could walk. Of course when I was that little my father was still with us."

"Would you like to go for a swim at my place before you go home for the night? Oh yes my pool is heated. If you don't mind the nip in the air between the house and pool it is a beautiful night. The moon will be up in an hour or so. It should be almost full tonight."

"What would I wear?"

"As much as I would like to say nothing, I have suits at my house," he said with a grin. "I'm sure one of them will fit you."

"I haven't done anything like going for a moonlight swim since I was a teenager. Let's do it!"

They locked up the museum and drove back to Kyle's house. On entering, Kyle lit a fire in the fireplace and showed Cynthia to a spare bedroom and a drawer with women's bathing suits. "You can pick out what you like and change in here. Would you care for a drink? Brandy or anything?"

"A brandy sounds wonderful. Why did you light the fireplace?"

"For after our swim. It's so nice to come inside and warm up by the fire." He stopped talking to grin at her. "Unless you're going to run home the minute we are out of the pool."

She gave him a mischievous wink and said, "I don't think so."

"In that case, I'll meet you by the fireplace with brandy and towels, ready to swim." He closed the door and went to his room to change. 'Tonight might be the night,' he thought. 'She is so beautiful, my snow angel.' He was happier then he had been in many years. Maybe he should forget about what he had planned to do. Maybe life could be good again after all.

Cynthia was looking through the swimsuits and wondering if they were ones Brenda had worn. 'Who cares?' she thought. 'I'm here now. Oh, I like this pink one—one piece with cutouts all around the middle—now if it'll just fit me.' She stripped and slipped into the suit. It was a designer suit—top quality. She thought it might be silk, as it was so soft and smooth against her skin. Looking in the full length mirror she was very satisfied with the fit. 'Now for the moment of truth—walking out to the living room with nothing on but this suit,' she thought with a smile. Cynthia stole one last look in the mirror—'hmm … not bad at all.'

She opened the door, stepped out and almost collided with Kyle, who was coming down the hall with a glass of brandy in each hand. He was wearing a pair of black trunks and a smile. "Wow! I almost had a brandy bath," Cynthia said with a giggle.

"Sorry sweetie, I was beginning to think you got lost in the swimsuit drawer." He took a step back and admired the way she looked. "It was worth the wait. You look wonderful. Ready for a bit of a chill? I was out by the pool to test the temperature. The pool's warm but the air will give you a thrill."

Taking a glass from his hand, she said, "I'm as ready as I'll ever be—let's go get wet!" She trotted down the hall and out the sliding glass door. Kyle was right behind her. She stopped at the edge of the pool, shivering. "It really is a little nippy on the bare skin isn't it?"

"Time to get in the pool," said Kyle as he stepped onto the water-covered stairs. "Ah, much better."

Cynthia followed his lead and in a few minutes only their heads and the hands holding their brandy glasses were above water. "This is fantastic Kyle, and look, the moon is just coming up above the trees."

"It will be full tomorrow night, Halloween. Speaking of which are we going to the party at the Sweetwater Casino? You seemed to think you could come up with a costume in time, but we really haven't talked about it."

"I'd love to go with you, Kyle, but I really haven't had a chance to do anything about a costume."

"You should go as my snow angel."

"Just what would a snow angel costume look like, do you think?"

"I don't know, be creative. Think of something. I'm sure a bright girl like you can come up with a beautiful costume in no time."

She giggled a little. "And what are you planning to go dressed as Mr. Dwyer? The snow king?"

His face broke into a big smile. "Well I have this big black cape with a red satin lining and most often when in need of a costume, I go dressed as Dracula. I von to bite your neck."

Cynthia thought, 'you can bite my neck anytime,' She said, "Dracula and a snow angel—we would be quite a pair. What time does the party start?"

"Usually about nine in the evening. But we could show up just about anytime. We could even go early and have dinner, with a beautiful view of the river. With the full moon it would be almost as beautiful as you are."

She smiled at his compliment and made a little swirl in the water with her empty glass. Just for fun she let go of the snifter and to her surprise it floated like a boat. Kyle stepped over beside her and let his empty snifter float next to hers. He smiled down into her eyes and took her in his arms, his lips brushing against hers.

Cynthia closed her eyes and felt a little dizzy as his kiss deepened, and she felt his bare chest press against her. 'Is it the brandy or his kisses?' she wondered.

He stepped back a little and hooking his thumbs under the straps of her bathing suit, started to ease them from her shoulders. Leaning his head forward he began a trail of gentle kisses down from her right shoulder along her upper arm following the descent of the strap.

She gasped just a little and realized that her breasts would soon be uncovered. She tightened her arms around him and snuggled against his chest. His chest hair was tickling her nose when suddenly he scooped her up in his arms and when he stood up she was completely in the chilly air. She slipped her arms around his neck, and shivered with the brisk chill of the night. He held her close and carried her up the pool steps and into the living room, leaving their floating brandy snifters to bob against each other with tiny musical notes. He placed her gently on the Persian carpet in front of the fire and took a big fluffy towel from the stack on a chair and wrapped it and his arms around her shoulders. Kneeling behind her, he massaged her shoulders and arms and started to kiss her neck yet again.

Kyle sat down behind her and leaned her back across his lap, in the crook of his left arm so his right hand could tilt her chin up to receive his hot kisses. Kissing her again and again, his right hand slid down the length of her body and along the outside of her thigh, gently rubbing back and forth from knee to hip.

She tilted her head further back so he could kiss her throat and neck. He slowly trailed burning kisses ever lower on her chest. Her excitement was rising and she was thinking, 'Tonight, yes, tonight,' when there was a huge crash from outside.

Startled, they both jumped to their feet and rushed to the front window. A bright orange ball of fire was reaching for the stars across the road from Kyle's house. He said, "Dial 911 and tell them there's been an accident across from 2269 Philadelphia Avenue." With no more explanation, he ran from the room.

Cynthia was on the phone with the 911 operator just a minute later when he raced back dressed in jeans, t-shirt, and boots. "Tell them we need police, fire, and ambulance," he yelled as he ran out the front door. She was just about to hang up when Kyle came back in the room with a young woman in his arms, both of them covered in blood. "Don't hang up."

Cynthia stood with her mouth agape at the sight of him. But she stammered into the phone, "Hold on—I have more to tell you."

He laid the girl carefully on his living room couch and said, "Tell them the ambulance should come directly to my front door—the victim is in here."

After Cynthia told the operator, she hung up the phone and said, "Are you all right? There's blood everywhere! She looks very young. Do you think she'll be okay?"

"I don't know. The car is totally engulfed in flames. No hope for the driver—he's still behind the wheel, poor bastard. She was thrown clear. Thank goodness she didn't have her seatbelt on. I found her on the ground maybe a dozen yards from the wreck. Go down the hall to the linen closet. Get several clean white washcloths, wet one with water, and bring them to me, please."

When she returned with the washcloths, Kyle pressed one to the girl's forehead where a deep cut was bleeding profusely. Then he turned to Cynthia. "Hit three on the speed-dial and hold the phone to my ear." After a few rings someone answered. "Butch its Kyle, listen buddy I have some bad news. There's been an accident across from my place ... yeah, I'm afraid it's real bad. The thing is, why I'm calling, well it's Janet. She's alive. I have her here in my house. No she can't talk, she's unconscious. Look I'm going to ride with her in the ambulance. Call Jake and Linda for me and have them meet us at the hospital." There was a pounding on the front door. "Look, Butch the ambulance is here. Gotta go, bye." He said to Cynthia, "hang up and let them in will you?"

As the paramedics came in, Kyle looked up from Janet's face. "Lauren and Kaitlyn—thank goodness the two of you are on tonight. It's ... it's Janet. Please be gentle with her. Please don't let her die." He stood and stepped away from the couch.

The paramedics worked on Janet and prepared to put her in the ambulance. Kyle and Cynthia stood by the front door. He wiped some of the blood from his hands and arms with a washcloth. "I'm going to the hospital with her. Would you mind seeing yourself home? I'm sorry the evening has turned out like this."

"It's okay; I'm a big girl, Kyle. I can get myself home. I do hope your friend will be all right. Will you please call me and let me know?"

"She's my cousin; that was her Uncle Butch that I called, so he can let the family know about what happened. I'll call you tomorrow morning to give you an update. Here they come with her." Kyle held the door open for the paramedics with their gurney, and its precious cargo.

SIXTEEN

He kissed Cynthia's cheek and then he was gone in the back of the ambulance. Cynthia stood in the doorway until the wail of the siren had faded into the night. She could see the flashing lights of the police cars and other emergency vehicles still clustered around the smoldering wreck on the other side of the street. With a shiver she closed the door.

She surveyed Kyle's living room and thought, 'how quickly things can change. One minute we're kissing, the next everything is a blood-covered mess.' She was cleaning up when there was a knock at the door.

It was a police officer wanting to ask questions about the accident. "Did she see it? Who was she? What were she and Kyle doing when they heard the crash, and so forth.

By the time the officer left, it was well past midnight, and Cynthia was exhausted. Pulling out of Kyle's driveway, she could see the flame-scarred tree across the street.

It was all that remained to attest to the tragedy. As she drove through town, she saw a cat sitting on the sidewalk. 'I forgot the kitty!' she thought. 'I must get cat food for him, but where at this time of night?'

She turned onto the Whitehorse Pike, and didn't have to go far to find an all night convenience store. Best of all, it was only about two blocks from her house. The young clerk was friendly and asked, "Did you hear about the wreck? Sean McCarthy was killed in a fiery crash on Philadelphia Avenue out near the lake a few hours ago. He used to come in here for cigarettes all the time. Man I can't believe he's dead."

In a shaky voice Cynthia said, "No, no I didn't know him." With two cans and a box of dry cat food she hurried home thinking, 'Sean McCarthy—that's the guy Kyle was talking about this afternoon. Always speeding around town.'

As she opened the front door of her house and turned on the light, the white cat came like a streak of lightning from one of the living room chairs. He began rubbing his head on Cynthia's feet and curling all around her ankles. "Well, it looks like you're glad to see me. Would you like tuna or beef? I got only two cans until we find out what you like." In the kitchen she spooned the tuna into a bowl and put it on the floor next to the cat's water dish.

The kitty was soon face down in the bowl, munching away and purring so loudly Cynthia could hear him from the kitchen chair where she sat. "My, you were hungry, and it looks like you really like tuna. You know what Kitty? I really like Kyle. I wish he hadn't gone with the ambulance. Of course I do hope the girl will be all right. That's his cousin Janet." The cat finished and sat by his bowl washing his face. "Just listen to me talking to a cat like you are a person. Oh well, I'm just tired I guess. Time for bed. Are you ready Kitty?"

Cynthia washed the empty bowl, and then picked up the cat. It licked her chin and she said, "Ooh! Tuna breath." But she nuzzled the side of the cat's head as they climbed the stairs to her lonely bedroom.

She was standing by the big window in her bedroom, still holding the cat and looking out on the moon lit night, when she thought she saw someone watching the house from across the street. It was more an impression then really seeing someone, but suddenly a figure stepped from the bushes across the street and walked away. "What do you think Kitty? Was that person watching us or doing something else in the bushes at one-thirty in the morning? I don't like it. Should we call the police? But what would I tell them? That we saw a person walking down the street? They would think I'm a fraidy-cat. No offense intended, Kitty."

She closed the shade and put the cat on the bed, then took a long straight white dress from her closet and held it up against herself. "How do you think this would work for me as a costume for a snow angel, pussy cat? Of course I don't have any angel wings or halo. We'll need to work something out if I'm going to be Kyle's snow angel tomorrow night. You know, Peggy might have an idea about how I can improvise something. I'll go see her first thing in the morning."

With a big yawn she put the dress back in the closet. It was one of her favorites and made of a clingy jersey material. She always loved the way it felt on her skin. 'Yes,' she thought, 'that dress, a pair of white pumps, with wings on my back, and a halo over my head. Kyle will have his snow angel.'

She put on her nightshirt, slid between the covers and was fast asleep when the kitty climbed up and settled on the bed next to her.

The moon was gone and morning sunlight was streaming in the window when Cynthia awoke several hours later. She stretched and sat up in bed, and then scratched the cat's head. "Good morning Kitty," she said brightly, "it's going to be a good day. I can just feel it."

The bedside clock read almost eight, two hours until Peggy opened her shop. It gave Cynthia just enough time to feed the cat, shower, and dress without rushing around like a mad woman and still get to Peg's by ten. Throwing back the covers she swung her legs over the side of the bed and was gripped by a strong stab in her abdomen. Grasping her middle with her arms, she thought, 'Not now! I've been feeling so good. Oh! I guess I shouldn't have stopped taking the pain medication Dr. Hicks had me on. I shouldn't have tempted fate. But I felt so good since I came back to Egg Harbor and met Kyle.' Cynthia stepped haltingly to the bathroom with an arm holding her side and took two pills from the bottle in the medicine cabinet. After swallowing them, she sat on the edge of the tub and waited for the pain to subside.

Two and a half hours later she was feeling fine and on her way to the florist shop. Her cell phone chirped. It was Kyle. "Good morning lovely lady. How are you today?"

"I'm ... good. How are you? How's the girl you took to the hospital?"

"She was lucky she was thrown from the car or she would have burned to death. As it is she'll be out of the hospital in about a week. According to the doctors, she should make a complete recovery. The driver wasn't so lucky. It ... it was Sean—the guy that almost hit my car yesterday afternoon."

"I'm sorry Kyle; I know he was your friend."

"Not so much my friend ... as someone I knew too well. It's very sad. But if you tempt fate often enough, it will catch up with you."

'Tempt fate.' The words echoed in her mind. 'I was thinking that about myself a few short hours ago.'

"Cynthia? Are you still there? Hello?"

"Yes, yes I'm still here. The connection must have cut out for a few seconds. Are you still going to meet Roy and me at the museum this afternoon to go visit his aunt?"

"Wouldn't miss it. Are you up to having an early lunch with me or if you haven't eaten, maybe breakfast?"

"I can't right this minute but in an hour or so lunch would be nice."

"Okay, how about I meet you at the Harbortown Diner, say twelve-thirty?"

As she parked in front of Peggy's shop she told Kyle, "Sounds like a winner. I'll see you then, bye."

He said goodbye and the phone clicked off just as she entered the shop. "Peggy, hi, it's me. I have a small favor to ask."

"Sure, you want some coffee? Or can't the favor wait that long?"

"Coffee sounds good. I hate to say it but I'm glad you don't have any customers, and we're alone. I need a pair of angel wings and a halo. Any ideas?"

"That's a little out of my department, Cynthia. Shouldn't you talk to God about this?"

They giggled together like schoolgirls. After throwing around some ideas, Peggy said, "You know, if you're going as a snow angel, you should have a big snowflake instead of a halo, and if I'm not mistaken, there is a certain high end lingerie shop over in the mall that sells angel wings."

"Oh my God, Peg, you are great! I knew you would have an idea about this."

"Yah, I can get pretty creative sometimes, and you know what? I have some large Styrofoam snowflakes from a display I did for Christmas last year. With a headband and a piece of wire it should look good. You're going with Kyle I take it?"

"Yes, I'm going to surprise him as a snow angel. Are you going to the party tonight Peg?"

"I am. I'm going with Ted. He's a bit young for me, but I really like him. We're going as a red rose and a white rose. My idea. I have this dark red taffeta dress with roses cut in the taffeta, and I found a shirt for Ted with a big white rose on it. With a green pair of pants he looks like a rose still on the vine."

"You mean Ted the pizza guy? He is very cute."

"That's him. I have been so alone since Tim died. I've known Ted, seems like forever. Then one day about six months ago he delivered a pizza here and it hit me how much I liked him. He was standing right where you are and I could just tell he wanted to say something. I offered him a cup of coffee, he sat here and we talked for almost an hour. When he left we'd made a date for him to come to my place after work and I would make him dinner. We've been seeing each other quietly ever since. Tonight is the first time we'll be together in a public setting, although we'll be in costumes. It is a Halloween party after all, so it shouldn't seem too strange."

Peggy had been working on the snowflake halo while she talked. Less than thirty minutes later, Cynthia was on her way to the mall to see about wings with a very cute snowflake halo on the back seat.

SEVENTEEN

Kyle was sitting in his car outside the diner when she pulled up beside him. He jumped out and opened her car door for her. "I was beginning to think you got lost in the wilds of Egg Harbor City."

"No, I just had some errands to run," she said while thinking to herself, 'Wait till you see your snow angel tonight, Kyle Dwyer.' "Sorry I'm a little late."

"It's okay. I feel I've been waiting all my life for you, what's a few more minutes? We still have time for a quick bite before we meet Roy at the museum." Taking her lightly by the elbow he escorted her into the diner.

Later, as they sat in a booth waiting for their lunch to arrive he asked, "So, what errands have you been so busy with this morning?"

"Actually, I was preparing a little surprise for you, but you'll have to wait until later to find out what it is. I think it went very well." She couldn't help smiling at being a little mysterious about things; after all it was Halloween. "Happy Halloween by the way."

"And to you. It's your birthday also, isn't it?" Reaching into the pocket of his sport coat he produced a card and handed it to her.

She took it from the envelope and was surprised to see a naughty little devil poking a cute little witch with his pitchfork. She opened it. It was a blank card and she read what he had written, "To my snow angel, may all your devils be gentle, and your Halloween birthdays full of love ... Kyle."

Her cheeks felt warm and she knew she was blushing. If you looked at it right it said, 'love Kyle.' "Thank you Kyle. You didn't have to, but the thought is sweet. Who knows? Maybe I will be your little witch, or snow angel, or something sooner then you think."

All too quickly it was time for them to be at the museum. Kyle paid the check and they were on their way.

They parked in front of the museum. Kyle opened her car door for and said, "Looks like Roy is here already. That's his car over there." The words were no sooner out of his mouth when they saw Roy came from across the street, waving.

"Good morning, Roy. Have you been here long? Cynthia and I are running a few minutes behind—sorry."

"It's okay. I was checking the water level in the serpentine—it's very high since we had all that rain. Can't hurt anything much anyway, except the picnic tables and they are pretty tough. If you two are ready we should get going. Shall we go in one car, or each in their own?"

"Cynthia and I are coming back here afterwards. So, if you don't have someplace else to go from your aunt's, we can all go in my Porsche."

"That would be great. I've never ridden in your car before, Kyle. Is there room for me in that tiny back seat?"

"Oh come on Roy, you're fairly slim and flexible and the back seat isn't that small. Not for just one person anyway. Climb in and lets go."

A few minutes later Roy said, "It's not that bad back here. Your car has a very smooth ride. I forget, when did you get this one, Kyle? It was right after Brenda left you, wasn't it? Such a sweet girl, I hated to see you guys break up. Have you heard from her at all? Somebody said she moved to California, is that true? I hope she's happy out there."

"Yes, I got this car right after she left. But it was on order from the dealer for several months before. Yes, she is in California, and no, I haven't talked to her in a while. I hope she has found happiness too. Now if that satisfies your curiosity about my personal life, what about you? Are you and Margaret getting married anytime soon?"

"Oh Kyle, you know Margaret and I are just friends. No need to get testy about my curiosity. After all, you and Brenda were together for years and years. Everybody thought you built your house just for her. She moved in with you right after it was finished. It's common knowledge you put in the swimming pool for her, then all of a sudden she's gone. You can't blame people for wondering. Cynthia, you wouldn't think he would be so touchy. After all, Kyle and I have been friends since our school days. The bullies used to pick on me and Kyle would stop them, if he was around that is. Didn't you Kyle?"

"Sometimes you make me wish I hadn't, Roy. But that was long ago, and we have all grown up, most of us anyway. Looks like we are going to be right on time. Did your aunt say if Jean and Frank would be there?"

"Yes, they will. Jean and Frank—now there's a couple for you. High school sweethearts, got married right out of school, half a dozen kids, I don't know how many grandchildren, and they are starting to get great-grandkids now. What a wonderful couple. Aunt Marie and Uncle George only had two kids, but Jean is a real gem. Of course it was such a shame about her brother dying so young. But those things happen. Now of course Frank is as close to Aunt Marie as any son could have been, even thought he's just her son-in-law. Oh, we're here!"

Out of the side window Cynthia saw a large brick ranch style house surrounded by big lawns, and what in summer must have been magnificent gardens. Tall trees let a steady shower of colored leaves rain gently down. It was a perfect autumn scene. "It looks like a Currier and Ives print, how beautiful!"

"Yes, I have always loved Aunt Marie's house; they have the best garden. You should see them in the spring when it is all just coming in bloom. The colors are just wonderful. Kyle, park over in the driveway. We'll use the back door and go in through the kitchen. That way we can see what Jean might have made for us to enjoy later."

"Roy, you are something else, I'll tell ya. Is that why you came down today? To see what treats Jean will put out."

"Shut up Kyle, you are such a prude. Let's just go in shall we."

Kyle held the car door and helped Cynthia out, while Roy went up and rang the back doorbell.

Cynthia and Kyle were just stepping onto the back porch, when the door was opened by a lovely tall woman in white slacks and a pale blue blouse. Roy said, "Jean, how are you? You know Kyle of course, and this is his friend Cynthia. She is interested in her family history and Dr. Smith and things. We're hoping Aunt Marie can shed some light in dark history corners like she so often does." As he squeezed past Jean, they heard him say, "Frank, how are you?"

Smiling at them, Jean said, "Same old Roy. Chatters so much you can't get a word in edgewise. Hi, Kyle nice to see you again, and you're Cynthia is it? I'm Jean. Welcome to our home, please come in."

She led the way into a big, warm country kitchen. "This is my husband, Frank. Frank this is Cynthia … I didn't catch your last name dear, I'm sorry."

"Dobbs. Cynthia Dobbs and it so nice to meet both of you."

She was impressed when Frank kissed her hand instead of shaking it. "A real pleasure to meet you," he said. "Come on in the living room and meet Marie. She is one of the sharpest hundred year old people you've ever met."

As he led them into the living room Cynthia saw one of the most regal elderly women she had ever encountered. "Come sit by me my dear. You are the young lady they have been telling me about, who wants to meet me and find out what I know about Dr. Smith, are you not?"

"I am, I ..."

"You're Elizabeth Stanton's granddaughter. They tell many stories about Elizabeth. How she and the others danced naked in the moonlight behind her house where there are thirteen hemlock trees in a large circle. Some say she was a witch. Is it true, do you think?"

"I'm sorry," Cynthia said coldly, "I came here to meet you, not to be insulted about my family. Gran was not a witch and I resent your saying so. Kyle can we go please?"

"Sit down my dear. I did not mean to imply that your grandmother was a witch. I only said that is what people say. I knew Lizzy quite well when we were younger. She was no witch! And you—I held you in my arms when you were a baby. You have your grandmother's fire. I like that. Do sit down, please?"

Astonished, Cynthia sank into a large wing chair next to the elderly lady.

"You see my dear; Egg Harbor City is very old. I am very old and when you get old people talking, stories get told and retold until the truth is lost in myth. Your grandmother was a wonderful woman. We played together when we were children. I was a bridesmaid in her wedding."

"I didn't know that. What about Dr. Smith? Did you know him, or anything about his ... treatments?"

"I only met or I should say saw Dr. Smith one time. My next door neighbor, Katie's mother, worked as a cook at the sanatorium, and Katie, being her daughter, was allowed to swim in the serpentine stream whenever she wanted. What with Katie and I being best friends, I was often invited to join her. It was about 1919 when I was twelve. Katie and I were there swimming. It was summer, very hot, August I think. Yes, we were swimming and splashing around in the first long stretch of the stream closest to the side of the sanatorium when the door at the bottom of the stairs opened and this bowlegged little old man with a white beard down to his waist came out and stood there looking at us. I remember I thought later it was like he could look right into my soul. But it wasn't a dirty look like men can give young women. He had soft blue eyes full of kindness and understanding. Then he turned and went back inside. That was the only time I had anything to do with Dr. Smith."

"That's a wonderful memory. But do you know anything about his treatments or the cures that he did?"

"Well ... let me think. He made people walk in the water of course. That was his main treatment, but Katie said her mother thought it was strange how he served the meals, and the patients always had to have a small glass of his special tonic with each meal. They would have the glass of tonic; then dessert, then each of the items of the meal one at a time. For instance you would have; a glass of tonic, peach cobbler, peas, corn, and baked potato, and then some kind of meat with a glass of red wine. Dr. Smith was not big on meat. He thought it plugged up the system. By today's way of thinking, it seems he was right."

"But do you know anything about how he made the tonic or where he got it?"

"My dear young lady, you seem awfully interested in his cures for someone who is merely interested in family history, Egg Harbor City and Dr. Smith."

"I, well ... medical things have always taken my interest. I didn't mean to ask just about that. How well did you know my grandmother? I never heard that you were in her wedding? I don't even know where she was married. Of course, I know they were married in 1933, she and my granddad John that is. Where were they married?"

"It was a very small wedding over in Greenbank, at that lovely little chapel there by the river. John and his family were from Greenbank. Old stories tell that his family had been in that area working at the Batsto iron works making cannon balls and musket shot for Washington's troops during the revolution.

"It was a beautiful early spring day. I remember it so well because my husband, George, had just gotten a new car. It wasn't really new; it was from his father, old Mr. Weiler. He got a new car every few years, and he would let one of his children buy his old one cheap. Mr. Weiler was very generous with his kids. Anyway we had about five flat tires on the way to the wedding. It was like that back then; they went flat and you fixed them on the spot. We got to the chapel just in time. We could have been late, but it wouldn't have mattered. There were only about ten people there and five of us were in the wedding party, not counting Elizabeth and John of course. I remember Elizabeth was such a beautiful bride. She wore a simple white dress with spring flowers in her hair and pinned to the dress, with a small bouquet of roses to carry.

"It was all quite lovely. For the reception we had a picnic by the river—everyone had brought a dish of some sort. I have a photo George took with the old box camera we had back then."

"I would love to see that—my grandma when she was young. I only remember her when she was older. I'm sorry about how I acted when we first came in. But no one had ever said anything about my Gran being a witch. Please, will you tell me what you have heard?"

"First let me say again that she was no witch. Not the Elizabeth Stanton I knew. However my friend Hazel has told me things she heard about Lizzy and some other women dancing naked in the light of the full moon behind the Stanton place and they were made young again while they danced. Now I don't know about what might have been done there but I knew your grandma and she would never be a party to such goings on! So put your mind at rest on that score. And about Dr. Smith, I'm afraid I've told you all I know."

The others had gathered around the two women as they talked, listening intently. Now Roy said, "Fascinating, but Auntie M. what about the tonics? You can tell that's what she really wants to know."

"Well, as far as I know he made them himself. I'm sure no one today knows what was in them. If he had formulas he must have had them in his head, not written down anywhere. Of course he might have, you can never tell, but they would have vanished with all his other papers, as so much time has passed. Roy or Kyle would know if there are any of his writings at the museum. What about it you two, anything like that, that you know of?"

They both shook their heads, and Roy said. "We have many papers, but they are news clippings, ads and postcards. No hand-written or personal writings. You have already seen a lot of what's there Cynthia."

They sat in silence for a few moments and Jean said. "How about some tea or coffee and a piece of my hot milk sponge cake? I just made it this morning. We can sit in the dining room, and maybe while we eat, Mom will remember some additional things."

Later in the dining room Cynthia said, "That was sooo good! I bet it's sinful. Jean, wherever did you get this recipe?"

"From Mom, of course. And you're right—it's very rich. It has six eggs, milk, cream and two cups of sugar in it. But it's the way you combine the ingredients when you put it together that makes it so good. Took me a while to learn to make it just right."

Roy said, "Every time I come to visit, and Jean has made one of her hot milk sponge cakes, I feel like I've died and gone to heaven. So Auntie M., has this wonderful chat loosened your memory about any additional tidbits that might help Cynthia with her search?"

"I'm afraid not. Cynthia, I would think you could get a lot of your family history information from the diaries Elizabeth and her mother kept. I remember her telling me about writing in her diary every night and how she got in the habit from her mother, Emma, who Lizzy said, 'wrote down everything'. But let me go see if I can find that picture from Elizabeth's wedding day. I think it is with the family history things in my cedar chest." She got up and slowly left the table.

Frank said, "While Marie is looking for that picture for Cynthia why don't you tell us about your kids, Roy? Has your son gotten out of jail yet?"

"Yes, he has. He's been home for about two weeks. If it wasn't for that wonderful Asian wife of his, I don't know how he would get by. She supports him and their three kids from the small herb business that she runs through mail order and on the Internet from their home. Right now he's looking for work, and helping her with the herb business.

"My daughter, Lisa, is doing well, as always. She has been with IBM for ten years now. She and her husband, Stanley, just bought another house out on the west coast. That makes five houses besides the one they live in out in Colorado. She told me on the phone, that with telecommuting, they never need to leave home if they don't want to. Of course I wish they lived closer. But they love it in the mountains. Oh, here comes Aunt Marie. Any luck Auntie M.?"

"Yes, Roy. It was right where I thought it was. Here you are Cynthia; you can see all of us standing by the river. All except my George of course, he was behind the camera. Your grandmother is in the middle with the bouquet. Wasn't she a lovely bride?"

"I've never seen a picture of her as a bride, and she looks so young! Is that John next to her? He looks even younger then she does. It's a wonderful old sepia colored photo. Do you think it would be possible for me to have a copy made? It would mean so much to me. You know I always thought John was older than Gran."

"He was, by about ten years. Everyone always used to comment on how youthful John looked. But all the Stantons looked young. Even when he was killed in that boating accident in the fifties, he looked like a teenager and he must have been almost sixty then. He's buried out in the Stanton plot in the Egg Harbor City Cemetery. If you go look at his headstone you can get the dates and find out his exact age. Of course you can just have the picture, no need to make a copy."

"Oh, I couldn't. But I will have a copy made. Perhaps in the next day or two I'll have time and then return it to you."

Kyle said, "Speaking of time, it's getting a bit late, and we do need to get ready for tonight's Halloween party."

Jean said. "Are you going? Frank and I never miss the parties at the Sweetwater Casino. We're going as Fred and Ginger this year. You know how Frank loves to dance. It should be great fun. What are you two going as?"

"I am going as Dracula like I always do, but Cynthia's character is still a secret. She won't tell, will you sweetie?"

"That's right, Mr. Dracula, you'll just have to wait and see. But I do think you'll like it. Are you going to the party Roy?"

"Oh yeah, I wouldn't miss it. Now, as much as I hate to say it, Kyle's right—it's after five and we really should be going. By the time we get back to the museum, pick up my car, and I drive home to change it will be time for me to go pick up Margaret. We have these wonderful matching Green Goblin costumes we're wearing, you should see them—they are quite shocking. Ah, what am I thinking? You'll see them at the party. Auntie M., I promise pictures for you."

EIGHTEEN

Later, on the way back to the museum, Roy said. "So, Cynthia, what did you think of my Aunt Marie? Isn't she fantastic for her age? And she was in your grandma's wedding. What a surprise! Aren't they all just great? How about that cake of Jean's? I'll bet you never had hot milk sponge cake before? Wasn't it a great visit? I can't wait for the party tonight. Come on Cynthia tell us, what are you going as?"

"You will just have to wait and see Roy. You're very quiet Kyle, is something wrong?"

"Me? No, I was just thinking about what Marie said about your grandmother and her mom writing diaries. Don't you have some of them? If they wrote that much, you'd think there would be many of them in that old place where you're staying. I mean, it just stands to reason, doesn't it?"

"You would think so. But I don't remember Gran writing in a diary, and I haven't seen any anywhere. I know mom didn't keep one." But she thought, 'I didn't know about the metal box with its letters and gold coin either.' "I'll have to keep an eye out as I work at cleaning up Gran's old house."

As they parked in front of the museum, Kyle said, "Looks like Margaret's here looking for you Roy. That is her SUV isn't it?"

"Yes, that's hers. She must be in the museum waiting for me. She's been a member for years and she's a past president of the society too. Tell you what, unless you need to go in the museum, I'll lock up so you two can go get ready for the party."

"That's very kind of you Roy," said Cynthia cheerfully. "As a matter of fact I do need to get home and start to get ready." Stepping from the car she said. "What time will you be by to pick me up Kyle?"

As he walked her to her car and opened her car door for her he said, "I don't know, are we going to dinner first or what? How much time do you think you'll need?"

"You said we could eat at the Sweetwater Casino before the party. I just thought that was what we were doing."

"In that case I'll see you about sevenish. That should give us plenty of time to eat before the party gets going." He leaned in the open window and kissed her. "See you then."

Cynthia drove home with a million things spinning around in her head. 'Shower first. No, feed the kitty first then shower, shave my legs, do my makeup, dress. Where would Gran's diaries be if she really kept them like Marie said she did? And what about great grandmother Emma's diaries? They could be the ones I should be looking for. After all it was Emma who was treated by Dr. Smith in 1906.' As she entered the house, a white blur streaked across the room. The cat was very glad to see her.

She picked him up and carried him to the kitchen. "I guess you missed me didn't you? Well let's get you fed, and then I have to get ready to go out again. You know what kitty? I have a more active social life now then I did in Glenfalls."

As the cat began to eat, Cynthia headed up to her room. As she laid out her white dress and angel wings on the bed she thought, 'Kyle is going to love this getup.'

She was stepping into the shower when the cell phone chirped in her handbag. She didn't hear it, or the message Dr. Hicks left for her. It would sit like a ticking bomb on her voicemail until much later.

As Kyle was leaving his house to pick up Cynthia, he noticed the blinking message light on his answering machine. The message was from his lawyer, David, telling him the papers would be ready tomorrow and if they could meet Thursday morning he could sign them. Kyle called and left a message that Thursday morning about nine would be good for him.

After finishing her hair and makeup, she slipped on the white jersey dress; it was cool and very soft against her skin. With a look in the mirror she remembered that she couldn't wear a bra with this dress, as it made the soft, draping neckline hang all wrong. After removing the bra, she again stood in front of the mirror. The neckline came down in smooth folding layers of knitted white cloth in the old Roman style, making her breasts appear as soft white mounds with a rounded but very deep cleavage between them. With nothing on beneath the dress but her panties she thought, 'Kyle is in for a surprise the first time he dances with me tonight.'

Cynthia slipped the shoulder straps of the angel wings over her shoulders and arranged the headband of the snowflake halo on her head. She was very pleased with the snow angel she saw reflected in her mirror. 'Just a few last touches—my gold bracelet, pearl ear studs, and I think the narrow white lace choker Rick gave me when we were talking about getting engaged.' "There," she said to the silent room, "Mr. Dwyer I think you will be most happy with the way your snow angel looks tonight."

The cat came in and jumped onto the bed. Cynthia picked him up and said, "We match, kitty, all white." The kitty regarded her with big blue eyes and his little pink tongue darted out to lick her chin. "Oh, more kitty kisses!. You must really like the brand of tuna I'm feeding you." The cat started to purr like a little train engine and snuggled against her. She rubbed her chin on the cat's head. "You are very romantic, but mommy has to finish dressing."

She put the cat on the bed and was just stepping into her white three-inch pumps when the doorbell rang. Looking at the clock she thought, 'It's just after seven; that better be Kyle and not another phantom ringer.'

A minute later as she opened the front door, she gasped in shock at the very real rendition of Dracula that stood with a toothy grin on her porch. "Oh, Kyle, you look fantastic! You even dyed your hair and put it in a widows-peak. It is you … isn't it … Kyle?"

"I von to bite your neck. Of course it's me, silly. Talk about looking fantastic—WOW—that is some beautiful snow angel getup. However did you pull it together in such a short time?

You'll be the hit of the party—I guarantee it. My God, Cynthia you look like a real angel. Where did you find the wings?" His hands touched the wings as he took her in his arms for a welcoming hug. "Real feathers too! And I just love a choker on a woman, that white lace is perfect for the costume."

"Thank you Kyle. But just one little thing—could you take out your fangs? They make your voice sound funny." He did and she said, "Good, now I can give you a hello kiss."

They stood kissing in the doorway for a few minutes and Kyle said, "We really should be going. If you're ready of course."

"Just need to grab my purse and lock the door."

A short time later as they pulled into the Sweetwater Casino parking lot, Cynthia thought it looked like the owners had really gone all out with the decorations. Both happy and evil-looking jack-o-lanterns were everywhere, along with cornstalks, orange and black lights and crepe paper streamers. The river was sparkling in the starlight, as the moon would not be up for another hour. Heavy hemlock and pine trees hanging low all around gave the entire scene a very spooky look.

"Oh, Kyle this is just so right and haunted looking for Halloween! I'm so glad we came. Did you say they do this every year?"

"Oh, yeah. Every year, and every year they add more and the party gets bigger. It's a good thing we came early for dinner or we'd have to park out on the road. The parking lot is big but no match for the number of cars that will be here tonight. Well, look at this, we'll be only a few rows from the entrance." As she was stepping from the car Cynthia's angel wings got caught on the door frame. "I guess you should have taken them off like you did your halo," he chided good naturedly.

"They are a bit awkward but they're very soft, so sitting in the seat was like I was cradled in softness. But I guess you're right, I should have taken them off. It's easy enough—they just slip off my shoulders." Standing by the car, she adjusted her halo. "I think I'm all ready. Shall we go in?"

Kyle took her arm and they strolled up to the front door, where a doorman in a ragged top hat and tails—looking like a character right out of a Charles Dickens book—opened the door for them.

They entered a large room with an immense stone fireplace, in which a crackling fire merrily ate up large, blackened logs. Dark wood chairs and tables around the room were set with orange and black checkered tablecloths. On each table was a small jack-o-lantern with a candle flickering inside. More orange and black twinkle lights hung from the ceiling and walls where there were frightful looking lighted masks.

A hostess dressed as a pirate wench escorted them to a table in the center of the room. Kyle asked, "Could we have a table by the windows please?" With a smile that said she knew Kyle, she led them to a table with a beautiful view of the river. When they were seated she handed them menus made up as parchment scrolls with skulls and crossbones at the top. "We'll be ready to order in a little while Jeanie, but could you bring us two glasses of Merlot first?"

"Sure thing, Kyle. It looks like we'll have an overflow crowd tonight. It's a good thing you got here early."

As the hostess went to get their wine, Cynthia said in a sulky kind of voice, "You surely do know everybody. What's her story, if you don't mind my asking?"

"Not at all. Jeanie and her husband have owned the Sweetwater for sometime now. It was about to go under when they bought it and started giving parties on all the holidays. Of course it also helps that Ted, her husband, is a retired world-class chef. Jeanie pretty much runs the place and Ted is happy as a clam in the kitchen without the responsibilities of running the restaurant. The holiday parties were Jeanie's idea and it really brings in the people. Halloween is one of their biggest, but New Year's Eve is their top; they have fireworks over the river and people come from everywhere to attend. Maybe if you would like to, we can be here this coming New Year's Eve."

"If what I've seen so far of Halloween is any indication, I would love to come with you to their New Year's Eve party. Here comes Jeanie with our wine, and another pirate wench. Do you know her too?"

"Yes, that's Bonnie. She's been here at the Sweetwater forever. People tease her about being put in with the pilings when they built the place." Then he whispered, "Under all that makeup she looks like the Jersey Devil himself." He started to snicker.

Cynthia had to smile with him, and as Jeanie and Bonnie arrived at the table she could tell that Bonnie had to be in her sixties at the very least. But she was thin, and with the costume and makeup she made a passable pirate wench. Jeanie said, "This is Bonnie, your serving wench for this Halloween eve."

"Bonnie, how have you been? How are the kids, and the grandkids?" Kyle asked with a smile.

"They're fine and you're the same old Kyle, aren't you! It's Halloween and you're a vampire. Is it Dracula or Lestat this year?"

"Dracula, and this lovely snow angel is Cynthia Dobbs."

"Hi, Cyn! I'm Bonnie and if this guy tries to bite your neck, call me. I keep a wooden stake in the kitchen." They all chuckled. "Now what will we have tonight? Or aren't you ready to order?"

"I keep chattering away," said Kyle, "so, she hasn't had much chance to look at the menu. Why don't you bring us jumbo shrimp cocktails, and by the time you do we'll be ready." He tilted his head and raised a questioning eyebrow at Cynthia.

"I love shrimp. It sounds like a plan."

"I'll be back with your shrimp, and take your order in just a few. Need anything else while I'm back there?"

Lifting his glass, Kyle said, "I think were good." As Bonnie retreated to get their appetizers he toasted, "To you my personal snow angel."

Cynthia raised her glass, touched the rim to his and took a sip. "It's a bit sharp isn't it?"

"It's not Renault, but I like to think of it as tangy. Their house wine is from California. Of course it isn't screw top either!" Their laughter joined with the general crowd noise, as tables were filling rapidly.

Ted and Peggy walked over and Peg said, "Hi guys! The snow angel outfit came out great Cynthia. I love the halo."

Cynthia said, "You should," with a grin. "Kyle, Peggy is responsible for my halo and she helped me get the wings."

"Peggy, I am eternally in your debt. She is my perfect snow angel. The two of you look really good too. A red and a white rose. It's so original. Your idea Peg, right?"

"Yes—I'm a flower person to the bone."

"You take good care of her, Ted. You're a very lucky man to have such a beautiful flower all to yourself. I didn't know you two were ..."

"We've been the best kept secret in Egg Harbor for a long time. But we are breaking out tonight. Aren't we, Sweetie?" said Ted as he hugged Peg around the waist and kissed her cheek.

Kyle raised his glass. "I wish you two all the luck and happiness in the world. Few deserve it so much."

There was a bit of a commotion at the door and as they watched, a woman dressed in a skimpy red witch costume entered the room. Several people gathered around her and followed her to the bar. "Wow, I wonder who that was," Cynthia mused aloud.

Kyle looked Cynthia straight in the eye and said, "I believe that was my friend, Brenda. She must be back from California."

Peg said, "We'll catch you guys later." She and Ted started off in the direction of the bar.

"Brenda—wow," said Cynthia as she got an eyeful. "That's some outfit she's wearing. I bet her heels are four inches at least, and modesty is ... well, not her strong suit. Did she dress like that when you were living together? I'm surprised she didn't come over to say hi to you."

"She probably didn't see me back here by the windows. But I'm here with you, and what she does or doesn't do is no concern of mine. If it bothers you that she's here we can go. We don't have to stay."

"No, we don't have to go. My God, Kyle, I don't care who's here, as long as I'm with you. But does it bother you that she's here?"

"Not at all. Look, here comes Bonnie with our shrimp cocktails. Have you decided what you'll have? I think I'm going with the rib eye, house vegetables, and a baked potato with everything on it."

"I believe I'll follow your lead and have the same thing. But just butter with a sprinkle of salt and lots of pepper on the potato."

Bonnie placed their shrimp cocktails before them with a well-practiced flourish. Kyle gave her their dinner orders and said, "Bring us two more wines, when you get the chance Bon."

After she left to place their orders, Kyle pointed over Cynthia's shoulder and said, "Look there."

Cynthia turned and looking out the window saw a huge harvest moon just coming above the trees and its light beginning to sparkle across the river. "Oh, it's so beautiful!"

Watching Cynthia's reaction, Kyle said, "Yes, and from this angle it looks as though you have the moon on your angel wings. Would you like to change places so you can watch the moon?"

"I would, but then you can't see it."

"I, my dear, would rather look at you any day." They switched seats and Kyle was holding her chair when Jean and Frank came in. "Look! There's Fred and Ginger."

"Oh my, Frank really looks dapper in a top hat and tails, and that dress Jean is wearing is just awesome."

Frank spotted them and asked Jeanie to seat them next to Kyle and Cynthia. As they approached, Kyle said, "Why don't we slide that table up against ours and make it a table for four? They'll be pushing all the tables together soon anyway to open up more space for the dance floor. Besides, we don't get to sit with famous movie stars all that often. You guys look great. What a fantastic Fred and Ginger! That dress is just stunning Jean."

"Thank you Kyle, but I happen to know you tell all the girls they look fantastic, don't you? Looks like the DJ's not set up yet so it's still quiet enough to hear yourself think. Ooh, those shrimp cocktails look good." Frank helped his wife with her chair and said, "Well we will just have to order two of them as soon as Bonnie comes for our drink order. That is some pair of wings Cynthia. Do you fly?"

"As often as I can Frank. You make a great Fred. Kyle tells me you dance as well as he did too."

"I manage to stumble around the floor fairly well. Maybe later Kyle will let me steal a dance with you."

Jean said, "Frank and I won several ballroom dance contests in Atlantic City. Of course that was years ago. But we still step around pretty good. How do those wings go on Cynthia?"

"They really are quite comfortable. They just slip on my shoulders with these white lace covered elastic bands, and they almost match my dress. Look here comes Bonnie with our dinners, and I promise to dance with you later Fred."

Much later as they were finishing their desserts, the DJ started the dancing off with 'The Monster Mash.' The four of them were all dancing and Cynthia was pleased to see Kyle was as good with a fast dance as he was with the slower ones. The pace picked up a bit more with the next song—an old disco favorite, 'I Will Survive.' They proceeded to the Village People's 'Y.M.C.A." The dancers did all the arm moves, or tried to, and were laughing with each other as they did.

When the song ended and yet another fast one came on, the two couples took a break. Returning to the table, they sat with brandy and coffee, chatting about their costumes and commenting on others around the room.

The first real slow song, an instrumental, 'As Time Goes By,' started and as Kyle took Cynthia in his arms he was surprised and very pleased to note she couldn't have much, if anything on under her dress. The soft jersey material felt nice under his hands and as he held her close she put her arms up around his neck. Wearing three-inch pumps brought her to just the right height so they could dance cheek to cheek. They stayed on the dance floor through another slow dance, locked in a dreamy embrace.

When the music ended they stood together a few moments longer, then Kyle tilted his head back a little and kissed her on the lips—a slow tender kiss. The song, 'Puttin' On The Ritz,' interrupted them and they returned to the table. Jean and Frank were clearing the dance floor as other couples formed a circle to watch them dance. Kyle said, "You could almost believe they are Fred and Ginger."

Cynthia excused herself and went to the powder room. As she was touching up her makeup her cell phone chirped like a demented cricket. She answered to find it was a wrong number. She was about to put the phone away when she noticed there was a message waiting. She clicked on the voice mail and heard Dr. Hicks' voice telling her he had her test results and would she please call him as soon as possible. She snapped the phone shut and put it in her purse. Damn if she would have this wonderful evening ruined by her illness! As if to tell her the choice was not hers, a small pain tingled in her side. 'A cramp from dancing,' she thought.

As she returned to the main room she was shocked to see Kyle slow dancing with the red witch and holding her very close. A lump grew in her throat, and she sat at the table and downed the rest of her brandy in one gulp.

Jean and Frank could see she was upset. Of course they thought it was just that Kyle was dancing with Brenda. Jean whispered to Frank, "Why don't you dance with Cynthia now?"

Frank returned to their table and said, "Cynthia how about that dance you promised me?"

She gave him a weak smile and said, "Sure, Frank."

He helped her with her chair and they took to the floor not far from Kyle and Brenda. Cynthia certainly felt nice in Frank's arms and he appeared to wonder what was wrong with Kyle that he was dancing with Brenda. "How about we cut in on them, and you can dance with Kyle?"

"We could, but if he would rather dance with that witch, I don't care."

"Oh, I think you do," said the older man with a wry smile. "I also think Kyle is a fool for dancing with her. They were together a long time, but that's over and done with—he should be dancing with you. Come on."

Frank guided them next to Kyle and Brenda. "Kyle, let me cut in won't you? I haven't seen Brenda in years," he said with a huge smile directed at the woman in red.

Cynthia was relieved and very pleased when Kyle gave Brenda to Frank and took her in his arms, quickly moving them across the dance floor away from Frank and Brenda. "Thank you for coming to my rescue," he said sincerely.

"The way you were holding her ... well, it didn't look like you needed rescuing. Why were you dancing with her?"

"Because we have known each other a long time. You were away from the table and she came up and asked me to ... for old time's sake. This used to be our song ... long ago."

"Autumn Leaves? This was your song? Can we sit down please?" Just then the music ended, they stood for a moment longer. The theme from 'The Way We Were' started to play.

"Please, Cynthia can we continue to dance? It seems to be the only place we can talk alone, and I feel I need to explain in some way. I'm sorry if it upset you that I danced with Brenda, but let's not let it spoil an otherwise good evening. Brenda and I were together a long time—we're still friends. But not anything more than friends, and we never will be anything more again. She has just recently gotten married out in California. She came back here this week to empty a storeroom she had rented and see a few old friends. One of them suggested she attend tonight's party. She's here with Carol and her husband. I think you met Carol at Peg's shop the other day. Now, can we forget about her and concentrate on having a good time?"

"That nasty woman is here too! She's the one who has been saying my Gram was a witch! And, you still haven't explained how it was I rescued you."

"Brenda was getting a little weepy and saying maybe she made a mistake. I was trying to convince her she made the right decision getting married. She was hugging me tighter and tighter all the time. I think maybe she's has had one too many tonight. Now what's this about Carol saying your Grandmother was a witch?"

"At Peggy's shop! When I first met her, she said my house is haunted and Gram was a witch. She practically accused me of being one too. Then when I bumped into her out at Renault's wineglass museum she asked if I had tainted blood from my Grandma the witch. I don't like her at all. She is a small-minded gossip who is afraid of her own shadow."

"I couldn't agree with you more. She and her husband have more money than they know what to do with and they are both afraid of everything."

"Her husband's afraid of everything too?"

"Oh, the great Dr. Stan? Yah, he's afraid of almost anything you can think of. Goes to church every Sunday to pray to God to keep him safe. I don't think he prays much for Carol though. Most people in Egg Harbor think they hate each other. But of course in public they are the perfect couple. They're in politics and all the right clubs of course. Not to mention the church. Old Stan and Carol give lots to try and buy their safety from all things real and unreal."

"Can we go sit and ditch some parts of my costume? I would really like to get these wings off; they're making my skin sore where the straps are rubbing."

"Sure—I want to get rid of this cape myself. You will notice I lost my fangs before we even started dinner. If you'll let me I'll kiss your sore skin to make it all better."

"Kiss my skin? You just want to bite my neck. I know all about you vampire types. You know what I would really like, is a brandy Alexander and a foot rub. Are you up to it Drac?" Sitting at the table, Cynthia put her foot on Kyle's lap, and he slipped off her white pump and softly massaged her foot. Then stealthy looking around, like a thief in the night he kissed her toes at the edge of the table.

Just then Bonnie said, "Everything okay here? Can I get you anything?"

"Bonnie, dear lady, we need two Brandy Alexanders. Tell the barkeep to make them with B&B twelve year old and heavy cream."

"Are you going to drive home tonight Kyle, or float home on an alcohol fume carpet? You know after this one I have to cut you off?" said the older woman in a friendly yet serious manner.

"It's okay Bonnie. We're staying for breakfast by the river."

Cynthia asked, "What breakfast?"

"It's late, and the Sweetwater always serves the last few customers breakfast out on the deck before they go home. Don't they Bonnie?"

"Yes, it's a tradition—anyone after three a.m. gets breakfast on the deck for free. And it's almost four. Didn't you two notice, almost everyone else has gone. Only you and a few other die-hards are left."

Looking around they saw it was true. Even Jean and Frank had gone and the DJ was packing up his equipment. "Well then two Brandy Alexander's and breakfast on the deck Bonnie!"

"Okay, if you'll move on out to the deck, you'll find a breakfast buffet and a fresh urn of coffee. I'll bring your drinks. Now scoot."

Kyle stood, put his cape back on and after helping Cynthia with her chair, offered her his arm to escort her to the deck. Stepping from the door Cynthia shivered as the cold air hit her skin. "Brr, it's chilly out here."

"That's why they do this on the deck. Not many are hearty enough to stay very long in the brisk autumn night air. But there is a place by the chimney that helps hold the warmth, right over here. We can sit next to each other and wrap the two of us in my cape."

"Yes. Let's grab two coffees, sit down and share your cape before I freeze."

They were snuggled in the corner whispering and sharing tiny kisses when Bonnie brought their drinks. "You two don't need to eat each other, even if you are Dracula, Kyle. The buffet is right there and getting cold." She gave them a conspiratorial wink, and she was off to the inside where it was warm.

Roy and his friend came over and he said, "How did you like our costumes Kyle? They were a bit warm inside all evening but out here they're perfect, even with the headpieces off. Cynthia, this is my friend Margaret. Did you two have a good time? Did you notice Brenda was here? Did you see her? I think she looked really fantastic in that red witch outfit. Margaret said she couldn't imagine wearing those tall high heels all night. Didn't you Maggie? Well we're off; it's almost time for the sun to come up. You better be careful Drac, or the sun will turn you to ash. See you later."

As they walked away, Cynthia said, "He does chatter on doesn't he? He didn't even let us get a word in edgeways."

They chuckled together. "As long as I've known Roy he hasn't changed a bit. And he never seems to notice no one gets to answer him. Of course he doesn't seem to care either."

"Maybe he just asks questions to have something to say, not from a real interest in the answers. Let's get some breakfast, I'm starving!"

As they stood, the cape slid from her shoulders and she shivered. Kyle put his arm with the cape draped around over her shoulder. "Think we can get two plates full with three hands between us and keep the cape around us?"

Cynthia put her right arm around his back snuggling against him and said. "Not only that but I bet we can manage with only two."

Later, on the way home, Cynthia was almost dozing off in the passenger seat and Kyle couldn't keep his eyes off her. 'She is so beautiful. Dare I try with her tonight? I want to so very much. My precious snow angel.' He sighed deeply.

Cynthia opened her eyes and gave him a radiant smile. "Tired Kyle? Wasn't it a great night? I don't know when I last enjoyed Halloween so much. Thank you for taking me."

"Thank you for coming, and let's not forget it was your birthday too. You are … very beautiful Cynthia … I …" Words failed him. How could he say what he was feeling?

Cynthia saved him from needing to say any more, as they pulled into the driveway of the old Stanton house. "Would you like to come in for a cup of coffee before you drive home?"

He parked the car, turned off the engine and took her hand and looking deeply into her eyes said, "You know I do." Leaning forward, he kissed her, and then nuzzled her neck behind her ear. The scent of her hair was intoxicating him.

In a breathy voice Cynthia said, "Let's go in the house."

As they entered the front room she dropped her purse on the couch and the angel wings on top of it. He took her in his arms and in an instant all thoughts of coffee were gone from both their minds. As they stood there gently kissing, holding each other, Cynthia brought her hands up between them and untied the black ribbon that held the cape around Kyle's neck. It slipped to the floor in a rustle of satin. He was wearing a white tuxedo shirt with ruffles down the front, a black vest, and a cravat around his throat with a large red stone pin on its knot. It was a classic Dracula costume.

As her fingers worked at the knot, he kissed her nose, eyelids and forehead. He softly trailed the tip of his tongue across the top of her eyebrow, and down her cheek to nibble on her earlobe. With the cravat gone she began to undo the pearl buttons of his shirt, and the soft cloth-covered ones on his vest.

Working tender kisses down her neck, his lips followed the shoulder strap of her dress as it slipped down her upper arm. He let the tip of his tongue trail fire across the strap edge to the top of her breast.

As he did so, Cynthia was kissing his neck and spreading the shirt and vest to expose his chest and pull the clothes off his shoulders and down his back. When his lips touched the top of her breast, she shivered and moved her head down to take his nipple between her lips and gently nurse at it.

He trembled with excitement and as pink and gold morning sunlight brightened the windows, he lifted her in his arms and carried her upstairs to her bedroom.

As they stood by the bed, Kyle kissed her almost painfully hard on the lips, and his hands slipped the straps of her dress from her arms. When he released them, the dress plunged to the floor. With his arms lightly encircling her, he kissed his way slowly down her front, stopping for a moment at each breast for an open mouth kiss on each nipple. Then he moved further down to tickle her navel with a tiny French kiss, and at last he was on his knees before her.

Her hands were in his hair, hugging his head to her as he laid it against her flat tummy, and with his hands behind her, he slowly eased her tiny white lace panties down her legs, where they joined her dress on the floor around her white pumps.

As he rose to his feet, she stood naked before him in the morning light, wearing nothing but the tiny, white lace choker and her high heels. He whispered, "You are so beautiful, my precious snow angel. Oh, Cynthia!"

They stood face to face hugging and kissing, as Cynthia worked at his belt, unfastened his pants, and they too joined her dress on the floor. Kissing her way down his chest until she was kneeling before him, she could see how much he wanted her—how ready he was. She was just starting to slip his briefs from his hips when he took hold of her arms and pulled her to her feet. He murmured, "I want you in your bed, lie down with me."

So saying, he lifted her in his arms and placed her on the bed. Looking down at her he thought, 'She is incredible and my body is so ready for her. Oh, Cynthia how I wish you knew what a wonderful thing you have done for me.'

Cynthia raised her arms in welcome. He sat on the edge of the bed and removed the rest of his clothing. Turning his back to her, he slid his hands down her long legs and slipped one tiny white pump from her foot, and kissed each little toe as she ran her hands over his back. He did the same to the other foot and turning the rest of the way around, lowered his head to kiss her breast as he carefully lay down on top of her. She could feel his hardness pressed against her thigh.

Cynthia slipped her hand between them and taking hold of his love she slowly guided him inside her. He gasped in pleasure at the wonderful feeling of her body wrapped tightly around him. Relaxing his weight onto her she felt his hardness go all the way in.

Time passed and their passion rose ever higher until in a shaking, trembling moment they were in perfect rhythm, and they reached the peak together.

No thought of Mei Lin touched his mind. There was only Cynthia. His snow angel had made the physical act of love possible for him again.

They lay together in blissful happiness. The morning sun sparkling in the window and soon they slept. It was mid-afternoon when they awoke and without a word made love again.

Cynthia awakened again to a light tickling sensation on her cheek. She opened her eyes to see that the cat had joined them on the bed next to her pillow and Kyle was using the tip of the kitty's tail to tickle her cheek. He said, "Hey sleepy head. We have been in bed all day. Shall we get up?"

She put her hand under the sheet and then said. "I think we will stay right here until we do something about this problem you have."

"That's not really a problem, but I know you have the cure for it." But instead of rolling over on her like she expected, he pulled her on top of him. "Now you, Miss Cynthia are in charge, whatever are you going to do ... about my little problem?"

She smiled wickedly down at him, "Little it is not, sir." And they giggled and thrashed about so much the cat jumped off the bed and went to sit on the bedroom chair.

When they next awoke, the moon had replaced the sun in the window and the room was all silver light and black shadows. "I'm hungry," Kyle murmured.

"I'm not surprised! You have been working very hard, sir. Shall we get up and go somewhere for a bite of dinner? Or would you rather order in?"

"Me working hard? What about you? You seem to be an insatiable little minx." He tickled her side. She giggled and tickled him back and they wrestled around for a bit. He kissed her nose. "How about we get just a few clothes on and order pizza?"

"Capital idea. You go do that while I use the powder room."

Kyle put on his pants and shoes and went downstairs to find his shirt. Searching around, he found her cell phone in her purse under her angel wings. He gently held the wings to his face to catch her scent and feel their softness. He ordered a supreme pizza with everything and extra cheese, and was just starting a small fire in the fireplace when Cynthia came down the stairs in a long, red silk robe.

He stared at her, and thought 'how beautiful you are with your hair mussed and wrapped in silk—even in your bare feet.' He said, "I ordered one like we had the other night. It should be here any minute."

"What would you like to drink with it? I have wine or coffee or …"

"No more wine. I'm intoxicated enough just being with you Cynthia."

She gave him a shy smile. "Okay coffee it is then. Do we have enough wood for a fire?"

"I was just about to step out back and get some more. You make the coffee and I'll get the wood."

When he came back in the house with an armload of wood, he could smell the coffee and then the doorbell rang. "Pizza time I think." Sure enough when he opened the door there was Ted with his pizza delivery container. "I'll take that Ted, here you go." He handed Ted a twenty.

"Thanks Kyle. You … ah … movin' in here, or what?"

"No, Ted just visiting." Just then Cynthia walked into the living room in her red robe, and Ted gave Kyle a knowing wink as he headed for his car. "I think Ted likes you," Kyle said.

Giggling she said, "I think Ted would like any girl dressed the way I am."

Later after the pizza was finished, Kyle was laying on the floor by the hearth, with Cynthia sitting next to him tickling him in the hair on his chest. "I really should be going. It's very late and I have a meeting at nine."

Cynthia pouted. "You could stay, and leave early in the morning."

"It *is* early in the morning." She leaned down and kissed him; her hair made a dark silken curtain around their faces. "Besides," he explained, "I have to wash out this black hair dye. I know it takes several washings and lots of effort to get rid of it. They say it's temporary, but I know from experience it takes a lot of work to get it all out."

With out a word she took Kyle by the hand, and led him upstairs to her bathroom. Turning on the shower she dropped her robe on the floor and said with a smile, "Join me?"

He stripped off his clothes and stepped into a world of soap, hot water, shampoo and Cynthia.

Later he fell asleep, safe from nightmares, in her bed and in her arms.

NINETEEN

Many hours later, he was late for his meeting with David.

When Cynthia woke up she was alone. Where had he gone? The last two nights and a day had been like a dream from the land of romance novels. But now she was alone in her cold, empty bed. The clock said ten a.m. Then she remembered, he had some kind of meeting at nine.

She lingered in a hot bath thinking of Kyle and their lovemaking. 'Why couldn't she have met him years ago?'

With a cup of coffee in her hand after feeding the kitty she thought, 'I must return Dr. Hicks' call. I've put it off long enough.' She was hunting for her cell phone, just as it started to ring. That made it easy to find. "Hello?"

"Cynthia is that you? This is Mrs. Hurley. Hello?"

"Yes, Mrs. Hurley. This is Cynthia. What's wrong? Is everything okay?"

"Oh, Cynthia, thank goodness I got you. I've been trying to call your apartment but all I get is the answering machine. Then I remembered you had a cell and it took me a while to find your number. Thank God I found it."

"Mrs. Hurley, what's wrong?"

"Why, your mother's house. It's on fire! I called the fire department an hour ago when I saw smoke from the side window. I've been trying to get you ever since. Where are you dear?"

"Mom's house? On fire, did you say?"

"Yes, yes. Oh,Cynthia it's terrible. You must come right away!"

"I'm several hours drive away but, I will leave at once."

*   *   *   *

In a newly renovated old office building Kyle was sitting in a leather chair with a cup of fresh Columbian coffee, waiting for David to finish with his other client. They had the windows open and the cool autumn air was very invigorating. His mind had drifted to Cynthia and the wonderful time spent with her. More importantly he had slept for hours not once but three times with no nightmares. Even now he could remember how fantastic it had been. And his body had responded as though there had never been a Viet Nam or a girl named Mei Lin.

David's voice intruded on his thoughts. "Kyle? Hey big guy, you looked as if you were on Mars or somewhere. You okay?"

"David, yeah I was just daydreaming. You ready for me now? Sorry I was late."

"No sweat. Come on in the office. You want more coffee? No? That's fine sit, sit, I have all the papers ready for you. Nino faxed the numbers to me Monday afternoon, and the funeral home sent over a copy of the prepaid, prearranged funeral agreement you have with them. I drew up the trust just like you wanted. It's all in order just needs your signature in a few dozen places." He chuckled.

Kyle scanned quickly over the trust documents. It was just as he had asked for it to be. Yet with pen in hand he hesitated to sign. After yesterday with Cynthia did he still want to do this? He had doubts. Not a week ago he was sure he couldn't go on living with the nightmare. But now, well he could change it if he needed to, it was a revocable trust and even if something accidental happened to him it was still the way he wanted his estate handled. He signed, and initialed, and signed again. There it was done. "This is effective today?"

"As soon as you signed it. Only you can change it. I'll have two copies sent to you. I would suggest you put one in your safety deposit box at the bank and the other someplace in your house. Of course I'll keep the original on file here at the office with your other legal documents."

After leaving David's office, Kyle took a slow drive around the lake and the back way to his house. It was another perfect fall day; blue sky, colorful trees, the air as fresh and crisp as one could ever wish for. Walking into the kitchen he thought, 'I'm going to call my girl.' The thought brought a smile to his face. He dialed. He waited, and the smile slowly faded as the phone rang and rang. Finally her voice mail came on. Lost for words he hung up. 'I hadn't expected her voice mail. Where can she be?'

He had no way of knowing that in her haste to head back to Glenfalls, her cell phone was left on the bedside nightstand.

He changed into jeans and tee-shirt to do some work around the house. Later he sat staring at the noon news on the TV without seeing it. He called again, when her voicemail message finished he said, "Cynthia! Hi, it's me. I guess I just wanted to hear your voice. Call me?"

He wandered around the house; he cleaned the ashes from the fireplace. He raked some leaves in the front yard, and polished the chrome on the Porsche. At four in the afternoon he tried her number again. 'Where can she be? We didn't have any specific plans but I thought she would be home.'

At six p.m. he watched the news and had a sandwich with a can of beer. He called again. Then he got in the car and drove to her house. She wasn't there and her car was gone. He drove to the museum, then randomly around town. He didn't see her anywhere.

At eight-thirty he parked in his driveway, locked the car and went straight to his library and the liquor cabinet. With a fire burning in the fireplace he sat in the living room with a bottle of Glenlivet scotch, slowly drinking his way into the night.

At three a.m. the next morning he dialed her number for the sixth time in as many hours and listened once more to her sweet voice on the recorded message. He hung up, put the scotch bottle in the kitchen, washed the glass and went to bed.

Less then twenty minutes later he was in hell, covered with Mei Lin's blood, watching the life fade from her beautiful eyes. Sitting straight up in bed trembling and shaking he said, "Don't scream, don't scream … AAAAHHHHH!" Stumbling and shaking, he staggered to the kitchen. With very unsteady hands he reached for the scotch, knocking it into the sink where the bottle shattered with a crash. He held onto the edge of the sink with both hands, and lowered his forehead to the cool, stainless steel rim. Kyle slowly sank to his knees, and then down to sit huddled on the floor as images from a faraway green hell—a hell sprinkled with blue eyes—flashed through his mind.

*　　　　*　　　　*　　　　*

Viet Nam—1975. The DIA had the information. His contact, girlfriend, and lover, Mei Lin, was playing both sides of the street. They told him in no uncertain terms to put an end to her. It had to be him; no one else could get close to her. And as always, he did exactly as he was ordered.

So, he made an arrangement to meet her at their regular place, the hotel Khach San on TuDo Street, better known to the GI's in Saigon as 'The Street of

Flowers.' It was a steamy afternoon even by Vietnamese standards. He knocked twice. She opened the door. He held her, kissed her and looked deeply into her eyes, trying to see the treachery there. But all he could see were big beautiful blue pools of innocence. Their color a genetic gift from her French father. He kissed her again and as she closed her eyes he thrust the knife in her side, right between the sixth and seventh ribs, just the way they had taught him. Her eyes snapped open and she tried to pull away. He held her, covering her mouth with his—stopping her screams with his lips—and watched the life fade from her eyes. He pushed her backward onto the bed and held her down while the point of the knife did its awful work in her heart.

As if in counterpoint to the last beats of her heart, a chopper thundered overhead, shaking the hotel. The US pullout from Saigon had begun.

*   *   *   *

At eight he got up from the floor, made coffee and sat staring out at the morning sunlight. It was going to be another beautiful autumn day—for most people anyway. He rubbed his cheek. He needed a shave. He needed a shower. Hell, he needed help. He needed Cynthia. But most of all he needed to put an end to his nightmare.

So, he drank the coffee, took a shower and shaved. Later he took care of some paperwork and paid the bills that were on his desk. At about two in the afternoon he took the double barrel shotgun down from the mantle above the fireplace. "Maybe she was only a dream inside my nightmare," he said to the ten-point buck he had shot the first time his father took him hunting. After 1975, he never hunted again.

Kyle sat at the workbench in the garage and cleaned each piece of the gun, oiling and polishing the wood stock and long metal barrels. After he put it back together, he admired its clean lines and put two nine ball double-o buckshot shells in the chambers, then snapped it shut and clicked on the safety.

Taking his time, he carried the shotgun slowly, almost lingeringly through the house, and then out by the pool. He seated himself comfortably in one of the redwood Adirondack chairs and looked at his surroundings: beautiful blue sky, a few fleecy white clouds, colorful trees in their fall dresses, and not a breath of air moving a single leaf. Everything was very still—cool and quiet.

Positioning the stock of the shotgun on the concrete paving between his knees Kyle clicked off the safety and took the end of the barrels in his mouth. He felt his way down the stock, and placed his fingers on the two triggers. If he timed it just right he could get both barrels to fire together. Closing his eyes his fingers tightening on the triggers, he heard, TINK-TINK.

Kyle paused. He listened. TINK-TINK … tink. Kyle leaned his head back and clicked the gun's safety back on. TINK. 'What is that sound?' Laying the gun next to the chair he stood up and listened closely: TINK-TINK … tink. Walking slowly, listening carefully, he looked at the pool. Colored leaves covered the surface. The pool man hadn't come by to clean it when he should have. 'Lot of people closing their pools at this time of year keeps them busy and makes their service run late.' TINK-TINK-TINK.

He stood next to the pool, looking down. Two brandy snifters floated by the side of the pool, knocking together: TINK-TINK…. He whispered, "CYNTHIA! YOU'RE REAL!" as tears dampened his eyes. "I will find you my snow angel, and make you mine."

He had just brought the glasses inside and put the shotgun back over the mantle when the phone rang. He grabbed for it and heard Cynthia say, "Kyle? Are you there? Kyle?"

TWENTY

Late Thursday afternoon, Cynthia stood with Mrs. Hurley and the fire chief, surveying the charred remains of her mother's house. She had arrived just as the last fire truck was pulling away from the scene. "We fought it for almost five hours," he'd said, "but these old wooden houses burn like tinder once they get going, Miss ... Dobbs did you say?"

"Yes, it was my mother's place. She died about two years ago. Do you have any clues as to the cause of the fire, Chief?"

"We think vandals or kids maybe set the fire, but we won't know for sure until our investigation is complete. You can get a copy for your insurance when we finish. It could take several weeks though. Here's my card; call me if you have any questions. Good evening to both of you."

"Thank you, sir. Oh, Mrs. Hurley what am I going to do? There were so many things in that house that I hadn't had time to sort out yet."

"Well, dear first how about you come to my house and join Bootsie and me for a cup of tea? Calm your nerves and chase this awful autumn chill away. A body could catch their death out here."

"Thank you, Mrs. Hurley. That would be nice, and I really could use some warming up. It's been a very long day."

They settled in Nancy Hurley's warm, cozy kitchen with its hint of fresh baked cookies in the air. Pouring tea, she asked, "Where will you stay tonight, Cynthia? If you haven't a place, you can spend the night with us. Bootsie loves it when we have guests. Have a cookie, dear."

Cynthia took a fresh cookie from the plate. "Thank you for the offer, but no. I do still have my apartment over on Lakeview Avenue. I'll sleep there and tomorrow I have calls to make and I don't know what happened to my cell phone. Good thing I still have a regular phone on the wall in my place."

"You know I never liked those cell phone things. They're like the TV remote—always getting lost. In the old days you had to get up to change the channel or turn up the sound, but you always knew where the controls were."

*　　*　　*　　*

When Cynthia returned to her apartment she emptied the mailbox of two weeks of bills and junk mail. Carrying the mail and her small suitcase, she climbed the stairs to her second floor apartment. Stuck under the door was a notice that her rent was past due.

She dumped everything on the couch and hurried to run a nice hot bath. While the water was running, she poured herself a glass of Merlot. Thoughts of Kyle brought a smile to her face with the first sip of wine. Glass in hand, she went into the bathroom and added scented bath oil to the water, lighted some candles, and stepped into the tub. It had been a very long day. Her body ached and the hot water felt so very good.

About ten the next morning, sitting with a fresh cup of coffee, she called the insurance company to tell them about the fire. After doing the press one, press two finger-polka for a while she finally got a live person. They said they would send an adjuster to the scene in a day or so but they couldn't make any payout until the police and fire departments finished their reports.

Next, gritting her teeth, she dialed Dr. Hicks' office. She spoke to the nurse and after about a fifteen minute wait the good doctor came on the line. "Cynthia I've been trying to reach you for several days. Your test results are not good. The S.A. has spread to your liver and I really need to see you to discuss it. When can you come to the office?"

"Why? Is there something new we can try?"

"Well no. But we need to talk ..."

She cut him off. "Look, Dr. Hicks, if there isn't anything new to try, than there is no need for me to come see you. Frankly, I'm fed up with all of it! I've read all the information; I've had all the tests and treatments. Nothing new? Then no visit! It's a waste of time!" She slammed the phone down so hard the plastic cracked.

Cynthia took her frustration out on the mail, ripping open bills she couldn't pay and throwing junk mail in the trash. Then she cleaned the apartment till it sparkled. She had lunch and about two-thirty she decided to call Kyle. Just thinking of him and the wonderful love they had made gave her a warm feeling, like a cozy fire on a cold winter's day.

TWENTY-ONE

Relief flooded through Kyle at the sound of her voice. "Cynthia! Oh thank God. I've been so worried! Where did you go? I've been calling and calling ... I even went out looking for you."

"Oh, Kyle, I'm so sorry if you've been worried. I was going to call you on the way to Glenfalls but I lost my cell somewhere. Then everything is such a mess here. Mom's house burned down. I've been so upset. I should have called you last night, but I was exhausted. Please forgive me for not calling right away."

"Your mom's house burned down? When did you go back to Glenfalls? I couldn't help worrying. We had such a great time at the party and ... after ... then, well you just disappeared. When I called and couldn't get you I didn't know what to think. Are you coming back to Egg Harbor? I'm very sorry about your mom's house. What happened?"

"They don't know. Mrs. Hurley called me yesterday morning and I just grabbed a few things and flew back here. It's amazing I didn't get a speeding ticket. Unfortunately Mom's house is gone, right to the ground ... so many things lost ..." Tears overwhelmed her.

He could hear her sobs over the phone. "Cynthia ... should I come there? Is there anything I can do to help? Anything at all?"

"Would you Kyle? I need ... I need you to hold me. There are so many things I haven't told you and it is almost too hard to go on."

"I know exactly how you feel." It was too hard to go on. "I'll be there as fast as four wheels can carry me. Oh, Cynthia, you don't know how much I need you too. And … there are things I must tell you as well. I'll be there late this evening or sooner if I don't get stopped for speeding too many times."

This brought a smile to her face. "Hurry Kyle, but do be careful. I want you safe and sound, but mostly I want you here to hold me. Hurry, bye."

"Wait, wait. Don't hang up! I don't know where you are or your number or anything. Cynthia? Hello?" There was panic in his voice.

"I'm still here Kyle. I'm on Lakeview Avenue, number 2712. It's hard to find because there are two parts to Lakeview and it twists and turns so much. When you get to Glenfalls, go to the diner on Main and call me at 555-3266. I'll come meet you and you can follow me home."

"I'm beginning to think I would follow you anywhere. See you in a few hours?"

"Yes, soon. Bye."

"Bye."

Kyle was elated. He had found his snow angel again. Best of all, in just a few hours she would be in his arms once more. With a quickly packed suitcase in the back seat of the car, a short stop at a fast food place for a bag of burgers, fries, and two large cups of black coffee, he was on the road within forty-five minutes.

About five hours later he drove slowly down the main street. The Falls Diner was right in the center of town, along with an old church, the fire department, police station, and a few small shops that were closed for the night. Kyle ordered coffee and asked about a pay phone. He called Cynthia. She said, "I'll be there in ten minutes."

He sat in a booth drinking his coffee, looking around and he thought, 'A typical New Jersey diner, but it's not in New Jersey.' The thought brought a smile to his face. A few people were sitting at the counter and one or two couples in the other booths. He turned his head to look out the window just in time to see Cynthia's car pull into the lot and park next to his.

He stood as she walked through the door and rushed into his arms. Despite the stares of the other customers, he held her tightly and kissed her so hard it took her breath away. When the kiss ended he leaned his head back and looking deeply into her eyes, said, "I think I love you Cynthia, and I never want you to be away from me again."

*   *   *   *

As he kissed her again, her mind was racing. 'What is he saying about loving me? I can't say it back. But I do feel I *could* fall in love with him. What am I going to do? He doesn't know I'm dying.' As the second kiss ended, she whispered, "Can we sit for a minute? I … we … need to talk."

They slid into the booth and he said, "If it weren't for you I … I wouldn't be here. I was just about to … when the brandy glasses clinked together … I …"

The waitress approached. "Need anything honey?" she asked Cynthia.

Cynthia thought. 'What is he saying? Brandy glasses?' The waitress' words interrupted her thoughts.' She said, "Oh … yes, could I have a hot chocolate please? It's freezing out there."

"Hot chocolate. Anything else for you sir, more coffee?" The waitress gave Kyle a radiant smile.

"Yes, please, coffee," he mumbled, staring into Cynthia's eyes. 'What am I saying? I can't tell her I was about to pull the trigger on my life.'

The waitress left. "What were you saying Kyle … brandy glasses?"

He could see the confusion on her face. "I … I found them floating in the pool this afternoon and I was just thinking of you when you called. You know, the ones from the other night when we swam together."

"It was nice. Swimming in the moonlight with you was very special. You have a beautiful home, and the pool is truly wonderful. We must swim again sometime."

"You're going to come back to Egg Harbor then?"

"Oh yes! As soon as I get things straightened out here. I have a lot of digging to do at the museum. I don't think I finished even half the pile of papers and files you found for me to look through. Maybe we could …"

Just then the waitress arrived with her hot chocolate and the coffee pot to refill Kyle's cup. "Will there be anything else?"

Kyle looked at Cynthia. She shook her head. He said. "No, just the check. Thank you." The waitress put the check on the table and walked away. "Cynthia, I want … I want …"

"What is it Kyle, what do you want? Tell me?"

He looked deep into her eyes. "I want you, Cynthia. I want you in my life, and I never want to be away from you again." He reached across the table and covered her hand with his, then lifted her hand, kissed her palm, and held it against his cheek.

She thought, 'My God he looks like a love struck teenager.' But his tenderness touched her heart, and she realized she wanted him too—wanted to love him, and make the whole damn world with all its problems disappear. "Let's get out of here. Come on, you can follow me to my place."

She finished her hot chocolate. They stood and Kyle put a twenty on top of the $8.00 check. He followed her to her car and after he opened the door, took Cynthia in his arms kissed her, and held her so tightly that when he let her go she was very warm despite the chill in the air. "Follow me, the road twists around a lot, so stay close."

They arrived at her place a few minutes later. Kyle parked next to her and was there to open her door before she had even turned off the ignition. As she stepped from the car he grabbed her and kissed her again. 'He's being very passionate tonight,' she thought as she led him to the door of the apartment.

As they entered the apartment he pulled her into his arms and whispered against her lips, "Cynthia my angel." Then he was kissing her again and again. Their mouths and tongues were together as they tumbled onto the couch. Buttons, shirts, trousers, skirt, shoes all were off in moments. To Cynthia it seemed like years since she felt his hands on her body.

The time apart combined with the terrible stress of the last two days lifted them to a peak of passion that could only be lessened in one way. Her right leg was flung over the back of the couch, and with her left foot braced on the floor, Kyle entered her. She groaned with pleasure at the feel of him inside her, as his mouth pressed hot, burning kisses on hers.

Their passion for each other had built over the last days; they were desperate for each other's bodies, and this ultimate life-affirming act. Each had faced death in their own way. Each found the need and will to go on in the other's passion and love.

In a moment Cynthia reached her peak, arching her back. Kyle crushed her to him, arriving at his own release with her. In the shuddering aftershocks of the climax they held onto each other in the fading heat of their passion.

They slid to the floor. Kyle was on his back, with Cynthia against his side, her back to the couch and her head on his shoulder. In a few minutes with a wicked glint in her eye she said, "Care to move to the bedroom?"

Without a word he twisted around to his knees, lifted her in his arms and stood up. "Which way to your boudoir, my lady?"

She had a mischievous grin on her face and said, "Whatever do you intend to do to me in there? It's that way." She wrinkled her face up and kissed him on the nose.

Carrying her to the bedroom he put his face to her chest and teased her nipples with his tongue. He stood by the bed, slowly let her feet down to the floor, and just stood holding her body against his, kissing her tenderly the lips, eyes and nose. He ran the tip of his tongue back and forth, just touching her lips.

Between his ministrations to her face and the slight movements of his body against hers, her passion was on the rise when she realized something of his was rising too. Taking his hardness in her hand she lifted herself on tiptoe until she was able to slip him inside her. Then with a slight jump she wrapped her legs around his waist. They stood there, joined together by their love as she gently lifted herself up and down.

After several minutes of this, Kyle carefully eased them onto the bed, where they made slow passionate love for the next hour. After she had two very strong climaxes, they came together on the final one leaving them both exhausted and very satisfied. They slipped off to dreamland together.

The next morning, Cynthia awoke first and lay in Kyle's arms watching him sleep. She was just thinking, 'What a handsome man, how peaceful he looks,' when Kyle opened his eyes and smiled at her. "Good morning sleepyhead," she said brightly.

"Good morning, angel. Morning already? You know what? It's truly wonderful to wake up and the first thing I see is you. And I sleep; sleep so … peacefully with you. Maybe you really are an angel."

"No, sweetheart. I'm just a woman. A rather frail woman at that."

"Frail? Why would you ever say that? You feel quite substantial to me." He smiled and squeezed her very hard against his chest.

"Kyle, this is the worst possible time for me to find someone and be falling … I mean … maybe … but … maybe I am, and because it's you … I … I have to tell you …"

Kyle interrupted her stumbling sentence, and trying to lighten her obviously darkening mood, said in a joking way, "It can't be all that bad. What are you dying or something?"

She looked into his eyes with her bottom lip trembling, and as the tears started she whispered, "Yes."

"What do you mean, yes? I just found you! I'm falling in love with you. You look healthy. Cynthia please don't look at me like that. Talk to me! Oh, my darling, what is it your trying to say? Cynthia?"

With her face buried against his neck she mumbled through her tears, "Yes, it's true. I haven't got much time left. Just yesterday I talked to Dr. Hicks and he told me it has spread to my liver, and I have even less time, and there are no new treatments and ohooo …" Sobs overtook her voice. She lay shaking in Kyle's embrace. He was the first person she had told her deadly secret to. She felt a kind of relief to share the burden with someone, but a kind of terror too. Would he leave her like Rick did? Rick had only known she was ill, not dying. Now Kyle, after knowing her only a week, had the full truth. What would he do? With fear in her heart she lifted her tear-filled eyes to look at his face.

The tenderness and concern in his eyes told her he would not leave her. "Cynthia, whatever is wrong, we will find a way to make you well. I do love you, Cynthia; there must be something we can try. Now that I have found you I won't let you go with out a fight to save you. You must tell me everything. What is it? Cancer?"

His tenderness and statement of growing love gave her strength. "No, not cancer. What I have is called S.A. that's short for Secondary Amyloidosis. It has to do with my genes. They give me a predisposition to it. I think the bad gene is from my great grandmother Emma. She was from Sicily. Remember I told you I was on a cruise in the Mediterranean and had to come home because I got sick? Well it turned out I had Mediterranean fever. I got over that, but it often brings on the start of S.A. that's why this is called secondary, and both are, are … fatal."

He stared into her eyes for a long time with much sadness in his face. "I nearly ended my life this week because I thought you were gone, or were never real to begin with. I will not let you die Cynthia. I will follow you to the grave before I live another day without you."

"Ended your life? What do you mean? Why would you do something like that? Just because I didn't call for a day, tell me Kyle? Life is so precious! What are you saying—that a woman you barely know doesn't call right away after you sleep with her and you try to kill yourself? Talk to me! Tell me!" She sat up wiping away her tears. The covers dropped to her waist. 'How can he even think of throwing away his life when I am trying so hard to save mine?' "Tell Me!"

"I have this nightmare, and it won't let me sleep. I was thinking about ending it before I ever met you. Three nights ago when I slept with you in my arms, was the first time I have slept for more than two hours at a time in about thirty years … and … and you are the first woman I have made love to in all that time. You don't know the hell I have lived in for so long."

"What about Brenda?"

"Brenda and I are very close friends. We would have been lovers, married—together in some way—had a life, if it weren't for my nightmare. She's a strong woman and … and she loved me. She tried to be with me, helped me for several years, but in the end she left. You must believe me. Only with you can I make love and sleep in peace. I don't know why or what it is about you, but you give me peace. You give me hope, Cynthia. And I will not let you die, not before we have had a life together. Now tell me more about this S.A. thing."

"I can't believe you wanted to die. What kind of nightmare? Just how bad can it be?"

"For now just let me say I wake up screaming about every hour or so and it takes me a long time to calm down and try to sleep again. Now tell me about this disease."

"Okay. It's well ... you know, you sleep very still and quiet when we are together." She smiled shyly at him. "Have you heard about what they think causes Alzheimer's disease? Amyloid protein deposits in the brain? It's caused by the same amyloid proteins, but instead of deposits in the brain, although that can happen too, they build up in other organs. In some people it affects their nervous systems, or their skin, or maybe their respiratory system. In my case it affects most of my major organs; heart, kidneys, liver and spleen. The amyloid makes the tissues of the organs get hard like leather. Eventually they stop working and the person dies."

"I think I read about the amyloid things and Alzheimer's. This is caused by that too, and they have no cure for it?"

"No. The treatments are just supposed to slow down the progress of the disease, but it just puts off the inevitable. Eventually you die. In the meantime you have pain attacks that are very debilitating. They can come at any time and last for a few minutes or several hours. I had one Tuesday morning. I took some pain medication and got it under control. It could have lasted all day and ruined everything. Thank goodness it didn't."

She rested her head on his chest. He felt so warm and strong. They lay together in silence for a time just drawing strength from each other. "So, you say they have tried everything in the way of treatments, and they didn't help?"

"For a time they did, but lately they aren't helping anymore. All the reading I've done about S.A. says that's pretty much the normal course and when the treatments stop working it isn't ... well it isn't long...."

"Shhh, its okay." He rocked her gently in his arms, and kissed her tears away. "We will find something, somewhere—there must be a cure. I won't let you die, my love."

"It's so sad it's almost funny, because that's why I was in Egg Harbor City when I met you. I was hoping that it was S.A. that Dr. Smith had cured my great grandma Emma of, and maybe I could find out how. But I don't even know what she was suffering from, much less how he cured her."

"You mean you think a cedar water treatment from Egg Harbor from a hundred years ago might make you well?"

"It's a possibility. I'm pretty much out of options. I'm desperate Kyle! I have nowhere else to turn."

They snuggled for a bit. He gently kissed her lips, then again with more passion. They made slow lasting love for a long time. Afterward as they lay quietly, Cynthia whispered. "Tell me about your dream—your nightmare."

"Thirty two years ago when I got out of high school, I was going to be drafted. The Viet Nam war was on and many of my friends had already been taken. So I thought I would enlist in the navy before they drafted me."

"You must have been only seventeen or eighteen years old."

"Yes. After I had been tested and had the physical I was waiting to here about when I would be inducted, when I got a call from a man from the DIA"

"The CIA?"

"No. The DIA it's the Defense Intelligence Agency. Hardly anybody has ever heard about them. They do a lot of very dirty things around the world. But I didn't know that then. I thought it was like James Bond or something, very exciting for a guy right out of high school. Turned out it was more like Bond than I would have thought.

They took me for a month or two at a time for training. My family and friends thought I was away at a government sponsored work/training program. Nothing about the DIA was ever mentioned. They arranged for me to be rejected by the navy and exempted from the draft."

"This is what caused your nightmares?"

"Not exactly. What I did for them, well one cretin thing I did for them, is the root of my trouble."

"Tell me Kyle."

"It's very hard for me to talk about. It isn't anything to be proud of ... I ... well, there was this girl. A Vietnamese girl, her Name was Mei Lin. She worked at the French embassy in Saigon. She had been giving information to a DIA agent for sometime when he disappeared. It was only my second assignment; I was to take his place.

"It had been fixed so I would meet her at an embassy party. The first time I saw her I fell in love. I was just a kid really, only nineteen, and she was so beautiful." Kyle stopped speaking, lost in the memory.

"Kyle? What happened? Don't stop now. Please ... tell me!"

He was staring into the middle distance seeing a different place and time. "She was standing in the receiving line, welcoming the guests. When it was my turn I took her hand in mine, she smiled into my eyes and I thought my heart would stop. Never had I seen a girl like that. We spoke a few pleasantries and the line moved me away from her. I can't to this day remember just what we had said but the sound of her voice, like music, was locked in my heart forever.

"Later as had been prearranged, I asked her to dance. While I held her in my arms and we moved around the ballroom dance floor we whispered the code words that told each of us who the other really was. But I didn't need the words; I knew it was her, and I'm certain she knew it was me. By the time the evening was over a date had been set for us to begin our seemingly innocent love affair. A lunch date at a Saigon hotel, the hotel Khach San on TuDo Street ... a place I wish I had never heard of ... I ..."

"What happened then? It sure doesn't sound like much of a nightmare to me; more like a romance. What happened to the girl? Did she meet you, or what?"

"Yes, oh yes. She met me there, at the hotel. It was November, 1974. We had lunch. Then we walked along the street holding hands and talking. She suggested that next time we should get a room so we could talk safely. It would appear that we were just two lovers doing what lovers do. I left her on the corner and she kissed me on the cheek. The date had lasted all of about an hour. I was in debriefing for the rest of the afternoon. They picked apart every word and facial expression of hers that I could remember. Being new at this, I thought they were just being thorough. I didn't know what was really going on."

"And, what was that?"

"The short answer to that is they thought she was a North Vietnamese spy, and maybe a killer. I told you I was taking the place of an agent who had disappeared. They thought was that she might have killed him, or had him killed. In any event, I met her the next Friday night, same hotel but in a room on the top floor, room 409, on the corner of the building right below the roof. It was that day we really kissed for the first time. I was losing my heart and the debriefing was an embarrassment to me. I talked to my handler about it. He said everything was a lie and not to let my feelings get involved. I didn't know what to do. As it turned out I started lying to them about my feelings for her and just gave them whatever information she told me. Of course there was information that I passed to her also on their instructions. I didn't know they were testing her to see if she was a double agent.

"A few months had passed, and Mei Lin and I were really in love, and our times together in room 409 got longer and longer. She told me she hoped to come to the U.S. someday when the war was over. By that time I was so in love, I asked her to marry me and said I would take her to the U.S.A. as my war bride."

"If you were so in love with her and had asked her to marry you, what went wrong?"

"The war, everything, you name it. It was 05:00 hours April 29, 1975. My handler and his people showed me scenes from a very bloody ambush in the jungle. Many of our boys were slaughtered like cattle hanging in a butcher shop. They told me this was the final nail in Mei Lin's coffin. This attack and loss was directly linked to information I had given her two weeks before. I stared at the photos that were green and red—there didn't seem to be any other colors but jungle and blood. Our young GI's had been killed because of information I had passed to her. But the DIA didn't care about those boys, only that this proved Mei Lin's treachery...."

Kyle stopped speaking. He was seeing something in his mind, not the room, not Cynthia, not anything here and now.

"Kyle ... it must have been horrible for you."

"Those pictures ... the ones of the slaughtered soldiers ... they are a big part of my nightmare." Cynthia held his head against her chest, rocked him gently, and said, "How can people be so cold? To throw away young lives ... to test ... to find out ... it's such a waste!"

The phone interrupted them. "Maybe you better answer that," said Kyle. "It's almost noon and you do have many things to take care of ... to get settled."

"Okay, I'll be right back." She got up and pulled a robe around her as she hurried to the kitchen to answer the still-ringing phone.

After a few minutes, Kyle got up and followed her to the kitchen, completely nude. He stood behind her and wrapped her in his arms as she hung up. "What is it angel?"

"That was Dr. Hicks. He still wants me to come talk to him in his office. I can't see the point since there are no new treatments he can offer. I banged the phone down so hard yesterday when I talked to him that I almost broke the phone. Do you want some breakfast? I have frozen waffles and things in the freezer and I'll have coffee on in a minute if you want ..."

Kyle turned her to face him, and cut her sentence short with a kiss. Nuzzling her ear, he mumbled, "Anything is okay. Coffee sounds great. You feel so wonderful in my arms. I never want to let you go." Her robe hung open and his lips put tiny kisses slowly down her chest to her nipple.

Color rose in her cheeks and she gently pushed him away. "We must stop. At least for today or we won't get anything done. Please Kyle, oh, please stop."

He lifted his head, and kissed her nose. "You're right. Coffee and some breakfast. Then what?"

"I think we will go to Dr. Hicks' office and you can ask him yourself all about S.A. and he can say whatever it is he wants to say to me. Now, you first in the shower, and I'll make breakfast. Okay?"

He kissed her once more; then headed for the bathroom, leaving her standing with her robe hanging open in the middle of the kitchen.

*   *   *   *

After breakfast, sharing a last cup of coffee together, Kyle asked, "What did you do with the cat?"

"Oh, my God, the kitty! I forgot all about him! He's probably starving by now."

"Can he get out of the house?"

"Oh, yes. He knows how to use the pet door that's in the kitchen."

"Well, I'll tell you what, how about I call Peggy, have her stop by your place and leave a can of cat food out for him by the kitchen door one or two times a day until we get back?"

"Won't she mind?"

"You met Peg. She'd love to help. Besides I don't see anything else you can do. Of course he was a stray before, and I'm sure he can fend for himself."

"No! That would be cruel. I took him in. I have a responsibility to him now, even if I don't have a name for him yet."

"That settles it. I'll call Peg. You get yourself ready to go see the doc, and we'll be outta here in no time. I also need to call somebody to cover for me at the museum."

Half an hour later she was ready—dressed in slacks, a sweater, and a pair of black flats. She returned to the kitchen. Kyle was going through the stack of bills she had left on the counter. "What are you doing?"

"Sorry. They were just lying here, with this notice from your landlord right on top. Cynthia, I can help you with these if you'll let me. I don't know about S.A. but I do know about money. You don't need the added stress of being in debt."

"Thank you, Mr. Rockefeller," she said stonily. "I will pay my own bills ... I ... I ..." Her voice broke and the tears came flooding out. "I don't know what to do. I've been without income for months and the medical bills keep piling up and the credit cards ... and ..."

He rushed to her side and took her in his arms, kissing her hair, kissing away her tears. "Hey, hey. It's okay. Cynthia, hey, come on. Look, I would be dead and my assets gone to the museum by now if I hadn't met you. You saved my life.

In Asia they say if you save a life, that life belongs to you. I figure that includes whatever that life was worth before. So it's really your money. Besides I want you to get better and be with me for a long, long time. I don't care about any money, only about you sweetheart. If we are going to defeat this thing you must let me help any way I can. Come on, give us a smile."

She looked up into his face. She could see love and concern for her in his eyes. "Oh Kyle, we do make a pair don't we? If you ever try to kill yourself again, I'll kill you! Now let's go see Dr. Hicks." She smiled. He kissed her and they almost didn't leave to see Dr. Hicks.

When they arrived at the doctor's office the receptionist told them that without an appointment it would be a very long wait. But just then Dr. Hicks stuck his head in the door to the outer office and spied Cynthia. He stepped all the way in and took Cynthia's hand, saying, "Cynthia I'm so glad you decided to come." To the receptionist he said, "Charmain, I'm taking Cynthia in for an emergency consultation. Everyone else will have to wait."

Cynthia looked around the waiting room. There were a few people waiting, and she could see they were not happy with this turn of events. Well, there was nothing she could do about it. He was the doctor. She said, "Dr. Hicks, this is my friend Kyle. Kyle, Dr. Hicks."

The two men shook hands and the doctor led the way back to his office. "Cynthia, I take it Kyle knows about your condition?"

"That's why he's here. I want you to tell him anything he wants to know about it, and you did say that you wanted to talk to me."

"Yes, I do. I want you to start the treatments with Colchicine and Prednisone again. Just because the previous treatments are no longer slowing the spread of the amyloid doesn't mean the S.A. won't spread even faster without the treatments."

Kyle asked, "Just what is happening to her Doctor?"

"The amyloid proteins are building up in her organs, making them firm, rubbery, and enlarged. Just what causes amyloidosis is unknown. Amyloid is a waxy starch-like protein, when enough of it is built up in her organs she will die. Most likely from liver or kidney failure. Of course it has also affected her heart, and congestive heart failure is a real possibility in the future. In cases like Cynthia's that I have seen ... and read about, this is very rare. At the stage where she is now, it seems unlikely she will live much longer. I wish I could tell you something more positive. Of course there are the rare, and even ... miraculous spontaneous cures that happen with almost all diseases on occasion. But that isn't something you want to count on. In the literature on S.A. there are only two reported cases of spontaneous cures. One of them is questionable as to whether the patient even had S.A. or not."

"Spontaneous cures! Dr. Hicks, you never said anything about that to me before. You mean to say I might just wake up one day and not have S.A. any more?"

"Yes. But it is so very rare … it even happens with cancer patients but you don't see people sitting around waiting for it to happen, because in the vast majority of cases it doesn't.

Don't get your hopes up about this. And that is why I never mention it to patients. It gives them false hope. You need treatment Cynthia, not pie in the sky dreams."

"Dr. Hicks, when was the first case of amyloidosis reported?" Kyle asked.

"Well, Kyle that's kind of hard to say. In the old records from a hundred years ago and more there are cases of symptoms that are most likely it, but that was before it had a name."

"So, it is possible that Cynthia's great grandmother, Emma, had it and was cured by Dr. Smith in 1906?"

"Anything is possible. Do you have the records from this Dr. Smith that I could look at and see if the symptoms listed are in line with S.A. and what treatment he used?"

"Unfortunately, no written records exist that anyone knows of," said Kyle sadly.

"A pity. Sometimes things they did in the old days worked, like the hot, wet, towel treatment for polio in the 1940's and 50's. Few doctors believed in it at the time but many of the patients recovered. It was very, very painful but it seems to have worked. Even to this day no one knows why or how. But this is all academic. Cynthia needs to get back on the accepted treatment. I don't see anything else to do."

Kyle turned to Cynthia. "What do you think? What do you want to do? The decision has to be yours. I'm behind you all the way, whatever you decide to do."

She looked at Kyle's face. "I want to search for Dr. Smith's secrets. I believe it is my only hope, and I'm betting my life on it."

They left Dr. Hicks sitting at his desk with a bewildered look on his face. Out in the car, Kyle kissed her and whispered, "I love you, Cynthia. Where to from here?"

"Let's go by mom's house. I want to see if I can find anything in the ashes. They should be cold enough to dig around in." She told him how to get there and as they pulled up in front of the pile of rubble that had been her mothers house she began to sob quietly. Kyle leaned over putting his arm around her and they sat for some time, just looking at the devastation.

Finally they got out of the car and walked around in the soggy ground that had been her mother's lawn. "It's such a mess. Where can we begin to look for anything?"

"It was two stories. Did it have a basement?"

"Just a small space where the heater was and mom kept some canned goods on the side of the steps. Look, at least the garage survived. Being back by the end of the yard I guess it was far enough away so it didn't catch."

"The house looks like a total loss, Cynthia. I don't think we'll find much by digging through the ashes, but maybe there's something in the garage you can save."

"I don't know Kyle ... Mom just kept the lawn mower and gardening things in there. You know, just yard stuff. I haven't been in there in years."

"Well, how about we have a look anyway? You never know what you might find."

She led the way to the garage and reached above the lintel, retrieving a key. "Mom was forever coming out here without her key, then having to go back to get it. So, it got to be left here. We knew it wasn't really secure but what would anybody steal anyway?"

Following her into the garage Kyle said, "You'd be surprised. People will steal almost anything that's not tied down." He looked around the dim interior and saw all the gardening things Cynthia had said would be there.

Cynthia clicked on the light switch and things got much brighter. He said, "Power still on?"

"Yes, the meter is on a pole by the garage, not on the house, so I guess that's why. If it had been on the house I'm sure it would be off. What are you looking at Kyle?"

"Up there, on the rafters ... what's in the boxes?"

"I have no idea, rags, papers, old fertilizer maybe? I don't know. There's a step ladder; let's find out." Kyle held the ladder steady while Cynthia climbed up and tried to lift one of the boxes down. It was much too heavy and the cardboard was weakened from age and dampness. She lost her balance and Kyle caught her in his arms as the box crashed to the floor, spilling many small black books. "What on earth?" Cynthia said.

Kyle stood her on her feet holding her by the arms. "You okay?"

"Yes ... I'm fine but what are these books?" They each picked one up, and Cynthia read, "Diary of Elizabeth Stanton, June, 1958."

Kyle said, "This one is November, 1962. They must be monthly diaries. It explains why they are so thin, and so many of them. There must be dozens of them here. Look, here's one from July, 1965."

"Oh, Kyle this is wonderful! These must be the ones Marie was telling us about that Elizabeth was always writing in. I wonder if her mother, Emma's, diaries are here too."

"Only one way to find out."

The rest of the day was spent looking through the diaries, reading little snippets, retrieving the other boxes and organizing them by date. When they were finished it was dark outside and they had the diaries from April 1933 to July 1966. "Wow, almost four hundred little books. My Gran sure was a prolific diarist. Over thirty years worth here; I wonder where the others are. Maybe Emma's are here someplace too."

Kyle stood looking at her. The same thought was in both their minds. There was a big pile of ashes where her mother's house had stood. If the diaries had been in there somewhere, they were gone now for sure. "I don't know about you, Cynthia, but I'm starving. How about we go someplace for dinner? The diaries may be here somewhere or even back in Egg Harbor City. Tomorrow we can come and bring big plastic storage containers to load all this in, and take it to your apartment to work on. Whadya say? Cynthia?"

"Sorry, I was just thinking of all the hours Gran must have spent writing all of this. Dinner sounds wonderful! A shower and some clean clothes doesn't sound too bad either. But do you think we could take at least the oldest ones with us tonight? I mean Emma died in the forties, so her daughter might have written something about her in the oldest of these diaries."

"Sure, I can't see why not. Here's a box that's still in pretty good shape. Pick out the ones you want to take with us and after dinner we can get started on them at your place."

From 1933 to 1945 there were over one hundred books. They wouldn't all fit in the box, so Cynthia had to be satisfied with selecting a few from each year.

As they were driving back to Cynthia's apartment Kyle pulled into the parking lot of a large fancy restaurant. "Kyle? What are you doing? We can't eat here. We aren't dressed for it, and I've heard it's very expensive."

"Not to worry lovely lady. You could be in rags and you would still outshine any other woman, no matter how she was dressed. I'm in the mood for some really good, expensive food and wine. This place looks like the ticket."

As they entered the dining room the maitre d' approached them. Looking pained, he said, "May I help you?"

"Yes, two for dinner. How about that table by the fireplace?"

"I'm afraid that's reserved sir."

Kyle reached out and shook the maitre d's hand. "I'm Kyle and this lovely lady is Cynthia. We want the table by the fire, please."

The maitre d' glanced at his hand as Kyle let it go. As if by magic, the man's whole attitude changed. "Certainly, sir! I don't know how I could have over-looked your reservation. This way please."

A minute later he was seating them by the huge marble fireplace. "Jacques will be your waiter this evening. If there is anything else I can do for you sir, just let me know."

He had hardly left the table when Jacques and a busboy took his place. The busboy placed a silver breadbasket on the table, filled their water glasses, and lighted the candle. The aroma of fresh, hot bread tickled Cynthia's nose. "I am Jacques. It will be my pleasure to serve you tonight, said the waiter. "Would you care for a cocktail before dinner?" He handed each of them a leather-bound menu.

"A bottle of your best Merlot and a cup of coffee right away. Cynthia?"

"Merlot sounds fine, but a cup of hot coffee sounds wonderful." She looked up at Jacques.

"A bottle of Merlot and two coffees. Please look over the menu; we have a special tonight, Chateaubriand for two. I will return in a moment."

"Wow, what did you do to them Kyle? The way they are acting you would think we were royalty or something. Mom and I always heard about this place but we never got to come here."

"It's amazing how much influence Ben Franklin still has, even though he's dead."

"Oh, Kyle, that's way too much to give away."

"It got me what I wanted didn't it? Besides we need a little pampering, and believe me I can afford it. From now on you are not to worry about money at all Cynthia. Not one penny. I am going to take care of you and somehow we are going to get you well."

Just then Jacques returned with their coffee. He placed a tiny silver cream pitcher with matching sugar bowl on the table, and then proceeded to open the bottle of Merlot and pour a small amount into a glass for Kyle's approval. Kyle tasted, nodded, and Jacques filled their glasses, and then left them to decide on their dinner selections.

"So ... you are going to take care of me, huh?"

"Better than anyone ever has taken care of you before." His face got very serious and looking into her eyes he said, "I love you, Cynthia Dobbs." He raised his glass of wine. "To your health and long life."

Cynthia picked up her glass and touched it to his. 'I love you too Kyle,' she thought, but didn't say. She said, "To life." They sipped the wine. Her blue eyes examined him over the rim of her glass. "What looks good to you?"

"You do my angel. Oh! You mean on the menu." They smiled at each other across the table. "I was thinking oysters Rockefeller for an appetizer, and what do you say we have the Chateaubriand for two?"

"I've never had it. It sounds very good though, so I guess we'll have that. I think I want a shrimp cocktail for my appetizer." Holding out her glass, she asked, "Could I have some more wine, please?"

Kyle filled her glass. "Chateaubriand is like a very thick steak from the best cut of the beef. It's cut from the center part of what would be the fillet. It should be served with sautéed new potatoes, glazed baby carrots or sautéed mushrooms or some such fancy vegetables with a Béarnaise or Colbert sauce to top the meat."

It wasn't too long and Kyle was proved correct. Jacques sliced the Chateaubriand at their table. It was served with new potatoes, white asparagus, and peas in lemon-flavored butter, with a perfect Béarnaise sauce.

The food was excellent, the fire crackled, the wine warmed them, and they smiled at each other a lot as the evening passed. After a pastry so light it could have floated off the plate, and a last cup of coffee, it was time to go. Feeling all warm and cozy, they walked arm and arm out to the car. It was gone!

"Kyle! Where's your car?"

"I don't know! It was right here in the last spot first row. You remember when we pulled in; there were only a few cars. The lot's full now, but I know where we parked."

Hurrying back inside, Kyle grabbed the maitre d' by the arm. "My car is gone! We need to call the police!"

"No! It's all right, Sir. A Porsche, yes?" Kyle nodded. "The valet noticed you left your keys in the ignition and the car door unlocked. He moved it to the valet parking lot. If you go out and ask him, he will bring your car around."

"I left my keys in the switch? I never do that!" As they descended the front steps of the restaurant the valet parking attendant came over. "You took my car?"

"The Porsche? Yeah, you left the keys. I'm sorry. I was around back when you pulled in. But when I saw the door was unlocked and the keys hanging there I thought I better put it away. I'm sorry for the inconvenience. I'll have your car here in a minute." Without another word the attendant ran toward the back of the building.

"Well that bit of excitement stirred up the old stomach. I don't know about you Cynthia, but for me the faster we get to your place and I can hold you in my arms the better I'll feel."

He put his arm around her shoulders. She snuggled against his side. "I know just what you mean." As he kissed her cheek, the valet pulled the car up to the bottom of the steps. Kyle tipped him a twenty and thanked him for taking care of his car. A minute later they were on their way to Cynthia's apartment.

They settled at the kitchen table with the diaries spread out between them. Kyle opened a bottle of Merlot and they each picked up a book. After several minutes of reading and both of them saying things like, "listen to this" it became obvious that they needed better organization.

"Kyle how about I get us each a big legal pad to make notes on, and when we each have finished a book we'll talk about what we found?"

"I think that's a good idea, so we stop interrupting each other's reading. I think we should read books dated close to each other to help keep the time frame close when we discuss them."

"Yes. Good thinking." She dug around in a cabinet for a minute and produced a stack of yellow pads.

Kyle smiled. "You use a lot of these? Or are you running an office supply store on the side?"

"No silly. I use quite a few what with mom being sick and research on S.A., not to mention trying to keep the wolf from the door. Here have two." She resumed her seat across from Kyle.

For a time they sat in silence reading and making notes. Kyle kept peeking over the top of his book, looking at Cynthia. 'She is so very beautiful. I don't want to be reading. I want to be holding her in my arms.'

Cynthia caught him looking. "What are you looking at?"

"You. I can hardly keep my eyes on the page for wanting to watch your pretty face. Just a moment ago you wrinkled your brow in concentration and I wanted to reach over and smooth your hair back."

"That's sweet, but what you could do, if you can take your eyes off me for more then a minute, is pour me a little more wine, please."

Kyle stood and refilled her glass. Then he kissed the top of her head. She tilted her head back, looking up into his eyes. He kissed her lips. She slid her arms up around his neck. Their kissing took on more passion. Kyle lifted her in his arms and carried her to the bedroom. "Kyle, we need to work on the books."

"Tomorrow my love, tomorrow." The rest of the night was lost to passion's demands.

*   *   *   *

The next morning when Kyle woke, Cynthia was gone. He got up and padded to the kitchen. Cynthia was reading, with a mug of coffee in her hand. "Hi, sleepy head, there's coffee in the pot—help yourself." He kissed her good morning. "Tell me, sir. Do you always walk around naked?" She started to giggle.

"Only with you my love." And he kissed her again.

"Well, please at least put on some pants. This is most distracting."

Kyle returned to the bedroom and put on his robe. Back in the kitchen he faced Cynthia and said. "Better?"

"No, but not nearly as distracting. Or ... fun."

He got a cup of coffee and sat across the table from her. "Finding anything of interest? I hope so."

"As a matter of fact, I was just reading in the June, 1933 diary about Elizabeth and John Stanton's wedding. She would have liked to have a much bigger one, but the depression was on and there wasn't much money. It's pretty much like Marie told us with the reception by the river, and each of the guests bringing a dish of some kind."

"Nothing about Dr. Smith and his cures, tonics and treatments?"

"No. Not so far. Kyle, how am I ever going to find a cure for me? I don't want to die, especially now that I've found you." She looked so very sad. Kyle reached across the table and took her hand in his. They stared into each other's eyes, and she drew strength from him. "We need to find Emma's diaries, but where can they be?"

"We will, wherever they are! We will also find Dr. Smith's cures, and you will get well. I won't let you die, Cynthia. You are my love, my life. If you die, I will too. Today we will get the rest of the books and however long it takes, we'll go through every one. If the answer isn't here we *will* find it, wherever it is. Look at me, Cynthia." He stood and taking her hand, pulled her around the table. "We are going to make you well! If we have to move heaven and earth we will. I love you with all my heart. We must get you well. We must!" As he took her in his arms he crushed her against him thinking, 'Cynthia, you must not die. How can I live without you?'

TWENTY-TWO

Peggy looked at her reflection in the full-length mirror in her bedroom. 'I'm old, well maybe not that old. Ted is so young. Not that young but how I wish we were closer in age. I was ten years younger than Tim. Now I'm six years older than Ted.' The door chimes sounded. She went downstairs and opened the front door. Ted was there with a rose and his normal exuberance. "Just a little late as always," she said as she kissed him. No childish kiss this. Ted was a man. Pulling back she said, "Stop! I'll have to fix my makeup again."

"I don't care about your makeup. I just want to hold you, and kiss you forever."

"And I you. But we are going to Sunday brunch together. It's our first time out in public as a couple. Other than the Halloween party, but we were in costume then, so behave. We will have plenty of time for other things when we get back."

"I don't care about brunch. Or who knows we are a couple." He kissed her on the mouth again, deeply and passionately. "I love you Peg, and I don't care if it stays our secret forever … or the whole world knows about it today."

'Yes, secrets, so many secrets,' "You do know I'm in the flower business Ted? But it's still sweet that you bring me roses. On our way to the Vienna Inn I want to stop at the old Stanton place. I promised Kyle I would feed Cynthia's cat for a few days."

"Sure, it's only a few blocks. We can do that. It's very sweet of you to close your shop so we can have Sunday brunch together. When did she get a cat?"

"Damn if I know. And even I deserve a day off to be with someone special every now and then."

A short time later they pulled into Cynthia's driveway. "Spooky looking old place ain't it?"

"Yes, Ted, it is. Even in the daytime. Come on I'm supposed to leave an open can of food and some water by the side door." Ted got out and headed for the side of the house. Opening her own door and stepping from the car, Peggy thought, 'He could take a lesson or two from Kyle about how to be a gentleman.'

She walked up beside him and got a can of cat food, a bottle of water, and a small plastic dish from the shopping bag she had brought along. "Do you see a cat anywhere?"

"Nope. Here kitty-kitty-kitty! It might be in the house, who knows? This is the place where people say a witch lived. Was she related to Cynthia do you think?"

"Yes. It was her grandmother. Cynthia gets very mad if anybody says anything about her having been a witch. Good word of advice, Ted. Don't say anything about witches around Cynthia."

"Who me? Never. Besides, I kind of like Cynthia. She seems like a nice person. What was it they were supposed to have done? Danced around naked or some such thing?"

"I believe so. Somewhere back behind the house."

Ted started back in that direction. "Come on, let's take a look."

"Ted, I can't go back there, I have heels on. They'll get all muddy. Come on, let's go. The cat will find the food just fine."

Ted stopped as a thin white cat came bounding from the trees behind the house. "Look! Here is your charge now. Nice kitty, good kitty." The cat ignored them both as it started to eat with real enthusiasm. Peg bent down and stroked the cat's back. It started to purr even though it was still eating. "Must be a male cat," Ted said with a chuckle. "One touch of your hand, and he's in heaven."

"Stop it Ted. You're just jealous because I'm not stroking you."

He stepped up behind her, put his arms around her waist and with his lips by her ear whispered. "You're right; I don't want you touching anyone but me, Peg. Did I tell you how much I love you already today? Let me tell you again. I L-O-V-E you Peg with all my heart." He kissed her behind the ear, then on her earlobe, and as he worked kisses down the side of her neck she turned in his arms, put her arms around his neck and kissed his lips with a fire he felt only when she kissed him. No other woman had ever made him feel that way. "What about your makeup?"

"I'll fix it later. Now kiss me again and show me how much you love me." He kissed her hard and ground his hips slowly against her until she had to breathlessly pull away. "Wow, you are all man, Ted and I L-O-V-E you too. But we really should go or we'll miss the brunch."

As they drove away, a pair of big blue eyes watched them. When they were gone, the cat went back to his food.

They arrived at the Vienna Inn in plenty of time for brunch. As they entered they ran into Carol and her husband, Stan. "Hello, Peg! Hi, Ted! Are you two finally getting out in public? It's about time, I must say," said a smiling Carol.

"Hi, Carol. We've been out and about together before. We missed you at the Halloween party at the Sweetwater last week."

"We were there! But you know Halloween is the devil's own holiday. Neither of us likes to be out to late on that night. Right, Stan?"

"Yes, dear. It is best to be home on a night like that. Ted did you hear they found a woman's body in the river the next day? It's just dreadful."

"Yes, I did hear about that. But they say she was dead for several days before they found her. Isn't that so?"

Stan started. "That's true but ..."

Carol interrupted him. "Come on Stan, you know talking about that poor woman gives me the creeps. I don't know why you had to bring it up at all. Let's go. Ted, Peg, enjoy your brunch if you can after this conversation." In irritation she walked out the door. Stan put his hands up in exasperation and followed her out.

"Wow. I hope you will never treat me like that after we're married. Did you see how embarrassed poor Stan was?"

"Yes, Ted, I did. You will never need to worry about me being anything like Carol." She gave him a sly smile and asked, "Just when did you decide we are getting married?" Before he could answer, the hostess came up to take them to their table.

She seated them in one of the leather-upholstered booths against the far wall. They ordered coffee, and as glasses of champagne were poured for them, Ted spotted Jake and Linda at a nearby table. "I have to go ask them how Janet is. She's my second cousin."

She was pleased that he stood by the table and waited for her as she rose to go with him. She smiled and said, "You're related are you? I don't think I know them. Of course I've heard about them these last few days. It was their daughter, Janet, that was in that car crash wasn't it?"

"Yes, seems like the family's been in town forever. It was their daughter that was in the crash with Sean McCarthy. Did you know her? I felt really bad about Sean. I liked him, and he always had the hottest cars. But what a way to die! Man I can't imagine being burned to death. Your skin blistering up and turning black, the pain must have been unbelievable. He and Janet came in for pizza quite a bit. I don't really remember when I saw them last, but seems like ..."

"If you keep on about burning to death, I won't be able to eat. Now, do you want me to come with you to say hello and ask about Janet or not?"

They walked together to the other table. "Hello Linda, hi Jake. How you guy's doin'? How is Janet? I was so sorry to hear about the accident. I, we ... this is Peg ... she runs Town Florists. We ..."

Linda took Ted's hand. "Janet is home, and recovering nicely with the Lord's help. We put our faith in Him and He always is there for us. Our prayers saved her. The Lord would have taken her home, but we prayed and prayed, and our baby is going to be okay now with His help."

"I'm sorry Linda, but you know Kyle carried her from the wreck. Cynthia called 911 and they took care of her until the paramedics arrived. Then Kyle rode in the ambulance with her to the hospital and stayed with her until you arrived. If anyone deserves credit for saving her life, it's Kyle."

"Kyle deserves more credit than the Lord? I think not, Ted! Without the Lord's help she would be gone. Praise the Lord!"

Peg tugged gently at Ted's sleeve. Ted said, "We really should be getting back to our table. Tell Janet I said hi. Come on Peg."

"Nice to have met the two of you."

As they seated themselves again in their booth she said, "Man are they always like that? I can't stand people who shove their God in your face with every word."

Oh, yeah. They are very big in their church and they smothered Janet with religion when she was little. She won't go to church with them anymore, and I think it must have driven them crazy that she went out with Sean so much. They of course didn't approve of him at all. So where are Kyle and Cynthia that you are feeding her cat?"

"Someplace called Glenfalls. I'm not sure where it is exactly. Not to change the subject, but what else have you heard about the woman in the river? I hadn't heard that they think she was dead for a few days. Do they know what caused her death?"

"I was talking to one of the state cops when he came in for lunch. I know him pretty good. He loves our calzone. Anyway he told me the medical examiner thinks she was dead at least three days and that she was strangled."

"Strangled! That means she was murdered. Oh my God. This is turning into a most upsetting day. Did he say if they have any idea who might have done it?"

"No. He didn't say anything more about it. I think they know who she is but they're not releasing the name yet. Let's talk about something more pleasant. Like us getting married. Marry me at Christmas, Peg. What do ya say?"

"Ted, is that a proposal I just heard?"

"Yes, I think it was. Peg you know how much I love you. Be my Christmas bride?"

"Ted, I …"

The waitress interrupted her. "What'll it be folks? Something from the menu or the buffet?"

Looking into Peggy's eyes, Ted said, "I think we'll have the buffet? How about it Peg?"

She said, "Yes," and the waitress went away. "And yes, I will marry you, Ted." She thought, 'Oh my God, what did I just do?'

Ted did a double take, his mouth working but no words coming out. At last he managed, "Really? You mean it? Oh wow! What a day this has turned out to be! I want to tell somebody. Oh wow! Really Peg?"

Touched by his excitement she said. "Yes, really Ted I will marry you and be your Christmas bride. Where do you get these romantic ideas? Christmas bride? Oh Ted!"

He sat looking at her. "We'll have to make plans. Wedding plans! Oh, wow, oh gee. Oh, Peg, I love you so. Big wedding or small, what do you want to have? Hey, I know this really great lady florist where I bet we can get a really great deal on the flowers." Their mingled laughter startled several people at other tables.

"Right now, if I can, I think I need to eat something," said Peg. They joined the line at the buffet table. "The prime rib at the carving station looks really good."

"I think I'm going to have Belgium waffles, with all the sweet stuff piled on top," Ted said with a grin.

"I think you have the biggest sweet tooth of any man in history."

He poked her side with his finger and whispered in her ear "I love you Peg. Oh, look at that dessert table! You know what we really need to look for, is a ring."

"On the dessert table?" They laughed together softly.

"You know what I mean, an engagement ring for your third finger, left hand? So everybody will know you're mine, and how very much I love you. Maybe since you did take the day off, this afternoon when we are finished here, we could swing by the mall and do a little window shopping in some jewelry stores."

"Boy, you don't waste any time, do you? But I guess it wouldn't hurt to look a little. Just to see what we like."

After brunch they drove to the mall, where they strolled for an hour or more, while they looked in store windows, especially jewelry store windows. On their walk around the second floor Peg stopped them in front of a bridal shop. She was transfixed by a gown in the window made all of white velvet with white fur trim. But the thing that really caught her eye was that in the white velvet, around the waist were tiny rose designs embroidered in gold thread.

"Peg? You see something you like? I thought the groom wasn't supposed to see the dress before the wedding day."

"Oh Ted! I think that is the most beautiful wedding dress I have ever seen! I don't care if you see it on a mannequin, but if we are really going to get married, then that's the dress I want to wear for you, as your Christmas bride."

"My Christmas bride. Yes, oh yes." He took her in his arms and kissed her, much to the surprise and delight of several other couples strolling in the mall, who tried not to watch, but smiled quietly to themselves about the love that was so clearly being expressed.

Late that evening at Peggy's house, as Ted made a nice fire in the see-through fireplace between her kitchen and living room, and Peg fixed them a late evening supper, it started to snow.

He settled himself in her front bay window-seat across from the fire, with a table pulled up to his knees, waiting for her. She came in and placed an orange parrot tulip in a cut glass vase on the table, and then special champagne cocktails made with raspberries and white champagne. There were two succulent raspberries per glass, with the rims wet with raspberry liquor and dipped in sugar. For their late night snack, she had made thick French toast of challah bread with new Vermont maple syrup and tiny turkey sausages on the side. She settled herself next to him in the window seat.

He raised his glass in toast. "To you, my Christmas bride." They touched glass rims, sipped and started to eat. "This is very good. Where did you get the idea for it?"

"It's from a friend of mine, Hazel Mueller. Do you know her?"

"Yeah. I think she's related to Roy someway or other, but the way he goes on when you talk to him, who can tell?"

When they had finished eating and the fire was dying, Peg stood up, took his hand, and as the snow fell softly outside, led him upstairs to her bedroom. She lighted some candles and they stood together, kissing gently. Soft, tender kisses of love slowly became more passionate.

Holding her against him, Ted's hand found the zipper tab at the neck of her dress. An inch at a time, he eased it slowly down her back. As the neckline loosened he trailed kisses down her neck, nibbled her ear and he whispered. "I love you Peggy, so very much."

Leaning her head back she said, "And I love you, Ted." Her fingers worked at the buttons of his shirt, and his worked the catch of her bra. Suddenly the dress slid from her shoulders. Ted slipped the straps of her bra down, took his arms from around her and moved her arms straight at her sides. The dress and bra dropped to the floor leaving her standing in just her panties and heels. Peg shivered in the cool air. Ted bent down and lifted her in his arms, her dress hooked on the toe of her shoe. She kissed his cheek and wiggled her foot. With a sigh of silk the dress fell to the floor.

He carried her to the bed, and watched the candlelight flicker on her ivory skin. Placing her on the coverlet he quickly removed the rest of his clothes and lay down beside her. He rolled onto his side to take her in his arms, and happened to glance at the snow falling outside the window. Was that a white cat on the window ledge? He blinked and looked more closely. Nothing there but snow.

Peggy, noticing his look and the sudden tension in his body asked, "Is something wrong Ted?"

"No, it was just … I thought … I saw something outside the window. But I guess it was just the snow."

A note of fear entered her voice as she asked, "Something like what? A person?"

"No, no nothing like that. It looked for all the world like a white cat was sitting on the window ledge looking in at us. When I looked more closely it was just the snow. Don't be scared. You know how the snow can be deceptive especially with the candlelight and wind."

He went back to kissing her, but she thought, 'there is no wind tonight.' Then he was kissing the soft spot at the base of her throat; she was very sensitive there. She leaned her head back and all thoughts of snow, wind, and cats were gone from her mind as he traced hot wet kisses down to her breast. His lips and tongue were making her squirm with delight as his fingers slipped beneath the edge of her panties, inching ever lower until the tip of his finger touched her special place. Slowly, gently it slid within her. She gasped with pleasure.

His hand stayed there only a moment before it pushed along between her thighs slipping her panties down her legs. She bent her knees and he removed her panties and heels in one smooth motion. Moving into position on top of her he took her head between his hands, looked deeply into her eyes and whispered, "I love you so." He kissed her lips as she opened her legs just a bit. They were both so ready his shaft slid deep inside of her. "Oh, Peg you feel so wonderful. Oh, sweet, sweet Peggy, my love." They were wrapped in love's embrace for over an hour. Sated for now, they crawled under the covers and lay together, making soft kisses, tickling, and just enjoying the warmth of holding each other. As they lay together, watching the candlelight flicker on the ceiling, Ted whispered, "Are you happy, Peg? You make me so very happy, I could die."

"Don't say die, Ted. Yes, you make me happier than I have been in years and years. What about a date?"

"I thought we were already dating?"

"I mean for the wedding, silly. If you want me to be your Christmas bride, the date should be close to Christmas don't you think? That doesn't leave us much time. Unless you're thinking of next Christmas?"

"No, I mean this Christmas. How about the week before? And how big a wedding are we talking about, do you think?"

"Well, I had the big church wedding with Tim. So, small would be okay with me, but what about you? You've never been married before. How big a wedding do you want and what about your parents?"

"They don't get a say. This is my wedding and I'm not their daughter, I'm their son. Small works for me. Of course, you know I'll marry you anyway you want, big, small, or just … a Justice of the Peace. I don't care! I just know I want you to be my wife."

Looking into his eyes she thought, 'I really believe you do.' She kissed him. He kissed her. Then they made love again, and fell asleep still locked in a lover's embrace.

Peg awoke with a start. 'What time is it?' She looked at the clock—nine in the morning!

'But it's still so dark!' Slipping from the bed she shivered in the cool air as she looked out the window onto a world buried in snow. She shook the still sleeping Ted. "Ted … wake up! You should have gone home hours ago. It really snowed hard last night. I have to get to the shop! Wake up."

Ted sat up in the bed, looking for all the world like a sleepy little boy. "What time is it? What's wrong, Peg? What is it?"

"We overslept. I have to get to the shop. You should have been gone hours ago. Get up Ted! What will your parents think? Then it hit her. 'He's not a little boy, and I'm not a teenager.' She started to giggle then laughed out loud. Ted grabbed her and pulled her down on the bed. "What the hell," she said with another laugh. "Anybody can see we had a blizzard. I'll leave the damn shop closed today, or open late or whatever. I'm gonna be your Christmas bride and to hell with the rest." Ted's hot kisses smothered her words.

TWENTY-THREE

While watching the weather channel, Kyle said, "It doesn't look good. We might be able to get out of here and head for Egg Harbor City tomorrow or the next day, but not today." It was the second big snowstorm of November and the northeast was buried under a blanket of white.

"Looks really bad huh? I don't feel so good anyway. It's only Tuesday. We can wait. Come hold me in your arms in bed. I feel so safe in your arms, Kyle." She looked at him with big, sad, blue eyes.

"Of course, darling. But you know it's the Tuesday before Thanksgiving. We've been here more then two weeks. And you know, if it will make you feel better, I'll hold you forever and ever. When you're stronger we will try to go back home. In the meantime Nino has transferred money to my checking account and I have taken care of all these old bills of yours."

"Kyle, it's not necessary. Please don't pay them, they're not yours, they're …" She sagged toward the floor, and Kyle caught her in his arms. "Thank you darling, I'm so weak any more. Your snow angel is melting."

"Nonsense! We're going to get you well, just as soon as we get back to Egg Harbor. We will find the secrets of the museum—Dr. Smith's secrets. They must be there somewhere. We're going to find them and you will get well, just like your great-grandma Emma did a hundred years ago." She gave him a weak smile, and then closed her eyes. He picked her up and carried her to the bed.

Two of the monthly diaries from Elizabeth Stanton had hinted about her mother's treatments by Dr. Smith, but they raised more questions than anything else. One said, "Thank God for the great Dr. Smith and his magical waters! The other said, "Dr. Smith treated Mom for free, as he was supposed to be very rich and have chests of gold hidden away. He would treat certain cases that he found interesting without charge to the patient." Both references were from diaries written in the summer of 1933. It had taken Kyle and Cynthia most of the two weeks they had been in Glenfalls to work their way through all the diaries they found in the garage. Some were hard to read because the ink had run and bled through the pages.

When they had finished all of the books, they had a dozen pages or more of notes. After much talking they decided that the only helpful information they had gotten were the two references in the books from July and August 1933.

*   *   *   *

Kyle was looking out the kitchen window when Cynthia came in. "Did somebody make a fresh pot of tea?"

"Cyn, you're up! Feeling any better sweetheart?" She nodded her head. It melted his heart to see her standing there in her sleep shirt and bare feet, looking like a little girl. "You're right; I just made a fresh pot of Earl Gray. Want a cup?"

"Very much, and a kiss from you. I'm sorry I'm so tired all the time. But I do feel much better now after my nap. Is it still snowing? I can't remember the last time we had so much snow this early in the season."

"Not nearly as hard as it did last night. They say it should be outta here by tomorrow. Then clear blue skies for several days. I was thinking if you're up to it we could leave tomorrow afternoon and be back in Egg Harbor City for Thanksgiving on Thursday. Whadya say kid? Shall we give it a try?"

She took the cup of tea he had poured for her. Sniffing the warm aroma, she stood beside him and looked out the window at a world so bright white it dazzled her eyes. "Wow, we really got some snow, didn't we? Do you think the roads will be good enough by tomorrow to try to drive back?"

"If this ends in the next few hours like they say and the plow and sand crews work through tonight and tomorrow morning, I think by the afternoon we should be okay."

Late the next day they started out. The roads were mostly clear but the traffic was much heavier than they had expected, as it was the day before Thanksgiving. After dark on Route 40 they stopped for doughnuts and coffee to go. Kyle was leading in his Porsche and Cynthia following in her car. They had just crested an overpass and Kyle reached for his coffee when his car hit an icy patch on the

down side. The Porsche went into a spin, the hot coffee went into his lap. Then
the car went off the road into a huge pile of plowed snow.

Cynthia pulled to the side of the road jumped out and ran up to Kyle's car just
as he was getting out. "Oh, Kyle! Are you all right?" She grabbed him and hugged
him tight.

"I'm fine, I'm fine. Pants are a little soaked with coffee, but I'm okay. Hey kid,
it's all right. Cynthia? Hey, trust me—I'm all right. Engine won't start though; I
guess I need a tow truck."

"Kyle, I saw you spin and go off the road. I was so frightened. You're sure your
okay?"

"Yes, yes. Look, I'll lock the car and we can go on to Egg Harbor in your car.
It's only about another ten miles or so. We'll go to my house and call a wrecker
driver I know. He can bring me back here to get the car. I'll leave the flashers on
and I'm sure the car will be fine for a few hours, till I get back to get it."

"Well, all right. If you're sure you're okay."

"Yes!"

They got into Cynthia's car and less then half an hour later pulled into Kyle's
driveway. "Somebody cleaned your driveway and walks," Cynthia said in amaze-
ment.

"I have a service that takes care of it anytime it snows. Let's get in the house so
I can call Joseph about getting the Porsche picked up."

While Kyle called his friend, Joseph, Cynthia freshened up in the bathroom.
When she came out Kyle said, "Unfortunately it looks like it will be a few hours
till they can give me a tow, what with the snow and the holiday and everything.
How about while we wait I rustle us up something to eat? Do you feel well
enough to eat?"

"As a matter of fact, right now I feel pretty good. What do you have in that
great big kitchen to tempt me, Mr. Dwyer?"

"Well, there's me, of course." He gave her a mischievous grin. "But let us go
look and see what we can find, shall we?" She followed him to the kitchen where
he pulled down several kinds of soup from the cabinets. "There's lots of frozen
things in the freezer too. Whadya think? What sounds good?"

She opened the freezer door, looked inside, and asked, "Are those all steaks?"

"Pretty much, yeah, all kinds and cuts. Is steak my ladies pleasure? I can thaw
some in the microwave in no time flat."

"Good, how about a T-bone and baked potato?"

"Coming right up. Why don't you pour us a glass of merlot while I get the
steaks and things started?"

An hour later, after they had eaten and they were sitting by the fireplace in the living room, Cynthia said, "You know what? I should drive over to my house and check on it and the cat. You can stay here and wait for your friend, Joseph. After you get your car taken care of, call me. Then either you come to my place or if your car is still not running, I can come back here."

"As much as I hate to be away from you, I think it's a good idea. Let's finish our coffee and you can get going. I'll wait for Joe, and I'll call you as soon as he gets here to give you some idea of when we might be back."

A short time later, standing in the doorway, he held her coat for her and as she slipped into it he wrapped his arms around her and whispered in her ear, "I love you Cynthia. You sure you feel well enough for this?"

Turning around in his arms she kissed him. "I'm fine right now. It won't be but a few hours until we will be together again. Kyle, I will miss you till then. Please be careful getting your car out of the snow."

"I will." He walked with her to her car and held the car door for her. One last kiss and he watched her drive away.

TWENTY-FOUR

Cynthia was surprised to see the snow in her driveway all flattened and the back doorstep cleaned off. Then she realized Peg and Ted must have done it when they came to feed the kitty. Stepping from her car she called, "Kitty, kitty, kitty?" No cat came. "Well I'll find you when I do." Going in the back door she realized the heat was still turned way down. She was glad to hear the heater come on when she turned up the thermostat. She looked around—still no cat, so Cynthia opened a can of cat food and filled his dish.

As she walked upstairs to her bedroom to shower and change she thought, 'Man what a draft on these stairs.'

After her shower she was coming out of the bathroom in her robe when as if by magic the cat appeared by her feet and meowed.

"Well there you are. Did you find your food?" She picked up the cat just as the bedroom door banged shut. "Man that's more than a draft. That's more like a wind." She slipped into her house slippers and carrying the cat, went out in the hall. She could feel the cold air blowing on her damp skin. "Brr! What's going on kitty?" She followed the breeze to the attic door, and opened it. A blast of frigid air hit her in the face. Cynthia looked up the stairs, and clicked the light switch. No light. "Bulb burned out kitty? What-d-ya think?" The cat just looked at her. "Yeah, we need a flashlight."

She returned a few minutes later with a big three-cell flashlight. The cat was still in her arms as she started up the attic steps. They creaked and groaned. The breeze was blowing the lower part of her robe open and she was shivering by the time she reached the top of the steps. Dust and cobwebs greeted her light in the cold attic space. Looking around, she saw a hemlock branch sticking through a broken window at the far end of the attic.

Half an hour later she was back in the attic dressed in jeans, heavy sweater, and old sneakers. With a saw, hammer, some nails, and a big piece of cardboard she was ready to cover the window. She tried to reach outside with the saw to cut the branch off, only to discover she was too short to reach it. She looked around the attic for something to stand on and found several small steamer trunks. They were heavy, but she managed to drag and push one over to the window. She stood on the trunk and soon had the branch cut and the cardboard nailed over the broken window. As she stepped down from the trunk she saw the cat sitting on the floor looking at her. "What do you think kitty? Good job?" The cat got up stretched and rubbed itself against the trunk. "What do you think is in there pussycat? I guess since we're up here it wouldn't hurt to take a look."

Stooping down, Cynthia unsnapped the catches and lifted the creaky lid. In the beam of her flashlight she could see dozens of little black books just like the ones they had found in Glenfalls. With trembling hands she lifted one and opened it to the first page. In a murmured almost reverent voice she read, "Diary of Emma Schnee: May, 1910."

TWENTY-FIVE

Sunday evening, four days before Thanksgiving, Peggy and Ted were just leaving his parent's house after a lovely dinner with his mom and dad. They just had to show off Peg's new engagement ring and announce their planned wedding date. Ted had told his parents the day after he and Peg got engaged, about his plans to marry her and all about the fantastic day they had when he had finally popped the question.

As they drove away, snow was beginning to fall. "Look at the size of those flakes Peg! Looks like the weatherman was right. We're going to get the second big snow of the season this week. I can't remember when it has snowed so much this early."

"Me either. We don't usually get big snowstorms until like February, if at all. Let's go feed the cat before we go to my place so we won't have to go out in it again." After they fed the cat and were driving back to Peg's place she said. "I've been thinking, Ted, what would you say about asking Kyle and Cynthia to be our witnesses for the wedding?"

"You know, I was thinking about asking Kyle to be my best man. I guess it's true what they say ... 'Great minds work alike.'" They were still laughing as Ted parked in Peggy's driveway. "Boy, it's really coming down. I hope the guys at the shop can keep on with the pizza deliveries till closing, without me having to go help take care of it. Business really picks up when it snows."

They ran for the back door. As Peg stood fumbling with her keys, Ted thought how beautiful she looked all sprinkled with snow. The big white flakes were melting in her red hair. He suddenly took her in his arms and kissed her.

"Wow! Ted do you think that maybe we can wait till we're inside first?"

As she opened the door he scooped her up in his arms and carried her across the threshold. "Just like it will be on our wedding day," he murmured.

She kissed him. "I hope so. Now put me down Ted."

"I could just carry you upstairs."

She looked into his eyes and whispered, "All right."

He kicked the door shut as he carried her through the house, then kissed the top of her head and nuzzled her ear. Cold drips of melted snow tingled on his lips. "You are so very beautiful Peg. I love everything about you from your tiny little ears, and your slightly turned up nose to your big, deep green eyes. My God, I could lose myself in the depths of those eyes." As they got to the top of the stairs he put her on her feet and eased the coat from her shoulders, letting it fall to the floor. She angled her head up and his lips touched the dimple in her cheek, the point of her chin and the tip of her nose, coming to her mouth at last, for a deep kiss that left her breathless.

He stepped back and dropped his coat on top of hers. She whispered, "More, more Ted. Please?" Once again he lifted her in his arms and carried her to the bedroom. Moments later he was standing by the bed, kissing and touching Peg. They could feel each other's passion growing to a red heat. Ted's fingers working at the buttons on the back of her dress until it slipped from her and she shivered slightly in the cool air. "My turn, sweetheart." She slowly unbuttoned his shirt, unfastened his pants, and peeled the clothes from his body. Tumbling into the bed, they wrestled around until the only bits of clothing remaining were Peg's high heels. "Should I leave them on?"

"Sure, you can use them like spurs to drive me on!" He laughed as he slid between her silken thighs. A moment later they had both forgotten all about shoes of any kind. While they made love, the snow continued to fall so quietly, as if on little cat feet.

The next morning when they got up and went down to the kitchen, a deep fresh blanket of white covered everything in sight. "It doesn't look like anything but the snowplows are moving this morning Peg. You gonna try to open the shop?"

"It's still early. Let's see what it looks like in a few hours. After all it is still snowing and I don't have any big orders to get out today. If it slows or stops, maybe I'll open at noon. Now come here and show me just how much you love me." And so, leaning her back on the kitchen table, he did.

TWENTY-SIX

Shivering with the cold, Cynthia was still sitting in the attic, trying to read one of the diaries, when there was such a pounding racket from downstairs, she almost dropped the book. She got to her feet, and with shaky legs made her way downstairs. Boom, boom, boom—it sounded like somebody was trying to knock down her house. At the top of the stairs she could tell it was someone at the front door.

When she got there and opened it, Kyle burst in saying, "Cynthia, are you all right? I've been knocking and ringing the bell for ten minutes or more."

"Yes, yes I'm fine."

"No you're not. You're shaking and your lips are positively blue. Come here and let me warm them." He took her in his arms and was shocked at just how cold she felt. He placed a burning hot kiss on her cold lips and could feel them warming to his in more ways then one. His hands rubbed up and down her back as he held her against him. She snuggled there in his embrace, enjoying the warmth of his body. Even though he had just come in from outside, he was warmer than she. "What have you been doing to get so cold?"

"I … I was in the attic. Oh Kyle, I found the most wonderful thing—I found Emma's diaries!" she exclaimed in triumph.

"Really? The ones from your great-grandmother, back in the early 1900's? Is that what you were doing in the attic in the middle of the night?"

"It's not the middle of the night. It's—what—nine o'clock, nine thirty?"

"My dear, sweet Cynthia. It is one forty-five in the morning."

"I must have gotten so wrapped up in the reading that I didn't realize how time was passing. Did they get your car out?"

"Ah, Joe was later then we expected and then I tried to call you but there was no answer. When we finally did get the car out though she started right up. Porsche really knows how to build a car. She has a little damage on the right front by the headlight. But it's drivable. So I came straight here. Then when I still couldn't get you on the cell phone and I rang the doorbell maybe a hundred times I thought something must be wrong and started pounding on the door like crazy. My next move was going to be to break the window in the kitchen door. Or maybe I would have tried to crawl through the pet door like the cat."

"I can just see you fitting in the pet door. Magic is skinny and small and he just fits through it."

"Magic?"

"Yes, he comes and goes like a magic cat so I thought I would name him Magic. Whadya think of that?"

"I like it—it fits him—white Magic."

As if responding to his name the cat jumped on the arm of the living room chair and meowed.

Kyle put his hand down and scratched the kitty's head. "Good Magic. Good kitty."

"I don't know why I didn't hear the phone. It's right here—well—it's not in my pocket. I remember it was on the night table when I left for Glenfalls. I found it when I came home tonight. I was going to put it in my pocket. But then I got dressed in such a hurry when I found the broken window that ..."

Kyle held her to him and stopped her stream of words with a kiss. He kissed her eyes, her forehead and nibbled her cold earlobe. "Cynthia, you are still so cold. Come on, I'll make a fire in the fireplace and wrap you in a blanket. How about a glass of merlot? A little red wine to get the blood flowing and warm you up."

"Okay. Then after, will you do me a favor?"

"Anything that makes you happy and warm my love."

"Well, while I sit here by the fire with my wine and blanket ... would you bring all the little steamer trunks down from the attic? They have the diaries in them. After that I would like you to sit here and hold me."

Half an hour later Cynthia was warm and happy as could be sitting by the fire all wrapped up in a wool blanket. Best of all was she was reading one of Emma's diaries. Kyle came down the stairs with another small trunk. "Is that the last one? I don't remember any of these being here long ago when mom and I lived with Gram. I used to play in that attic."

"These are the very last," said Kyle. The only things still in the attic are a few cardboard boxes and cold air. Just to be sure, I looked in the boxes. There were old clothes, newspapers, and not much else. So this is the lot. Cynthia? Do you suppose you could spare a glass of your wine for a hard working man?" He had a mischievous grin on his face.

"For one as helpful and loving as you? I don't see why not. Besides, I did ask you to hold me when you finished. Or have you forgotten?"

"Forget to hold you? NEVER!" He poured himself a glass of wine and took a sip. Then setting it aside, he took her in his arms and held her so close she had to turn her face to his. Like a magnet to steel, his lips found hers. Softly at first, then with growing warmth and passion, and then the way she had come to love about Kyle's kisses, just the tip of his tongue between his lips sliding back and forth on hers. Rapidly their rising desire for each other grew from a candle flame to a roaring fire that consumed them both.

Afterward, lying before the fire wrapped in the blanket and each other's arms. Cynthia asked, "Kyle? Have you noticed you can feel the S.A. in my body?"

"What do you mean? Feel it?"

She took his hand and placed it on her abdomen. "Press down just a little with your fingertips right here, a bit to the left of my bellybutton ... feel it?"

"I ... I'm not sure. It feels like a hard lump ... but deep inside and yet ... somehow soft."

"Yes, and over here?" Kyle nodded his head. "That's where the S.A. has already hardened parts of my organs." Kyle's hand and fingers gently explored the surface of her stomach, softly touching and pressing.

She saw the firelight reflected in a tear on his cheek. "Oh, Kyle ..."

"Cynthia, it's just ... just I always thought that when I loved a woman like I love you ... and she put my hand on her stomach it would be ... it would be to feel our child kicking and growing inside of her." He held her in his arms, and they cried quietly together until they fell asleep. The only sound in the room was the dying snap and sizzle of the fire.

TWENTY-SEVEN

It was Tuesday afternoon by the time Peg and Ted got to open Town Florists. The snow was still falling but the road crews had plowed and sanded so people were able to get around again. "Now that your shop is open and running, I've gotta go get the Pizza Palace going or the family will kill me. Being closed yesterday when everything else was closed was one thing. Another day when things are starting to move again is quite another." He took her in his arms. "I love you so much Peg, I could just scream it to the whole world."

He held her. They kissed a slow, deep, loving kiss. "I'll see you tonight?" She whispered.

"As soon as we close, I'll be at your door."

"I'll be waiting." She watched him drive off into the mist of softly falling snow. She returned to the back room and had just started to unpack a box of tall vases when the front door chimed that a customer had entered the shop.

"Peggy, are you back there? It's me Carol. Hello?"

"Hi Carol. How are you and Stan making out with this weather? I didn't expect to see you out and about in this."

"I wouldn't be, but I need a fresh flower arrangement for my table tonight. We're having a few friends in for dinner. Isn't this weather terrible? Of course you and I know what's causing it?"

"We do? What are you thinking Carol?"

"Well, it's that witch being back in town. I knew as soon as I found out about her there would be awful things happening. Think of that poor woman they found in the river. Murdered on Halloween. It's that witch I tell you."

"I heard the woman was killed several days before Halloween. And just what witch are you talking about?"

"Why, I met her right here in your shop. That Cynthia Dobbs who is living in the old Stanton place. Right where her grandmother, the last witch, lived. She's the one! She's responsible for this weather … and everything else bad that has happened."

"Cynthia is not a witch. She is one of the nicest people I've met in a long time. You should be careful going around saying bad things about her. You might get sued for slander. Now, if it's about flowers, what kind of arrangement do you want?"

"Something … I don't know … something … bright, but not ostentatious, and not too big."

"I can show you some made up arrangements I have, or I have pictures of many other styles. You've been coming here for a long time. You know what we carry Carol."

"The one I had last year for the before Christmas, Christmas Party … something like that would be wonderful."

Peg looked in her records and found that Carol had purchased a centerpiece of white and red carnations with green ferns, sprigs of holly, and two white tapers in the center for her party last year. After talking about it for a while they decided to use the same one again but without the candles, as Carol had worried all through dinner last year that they would cause a fire. The candles were replaced with silver painted pine cones. Carol left the shop about half an hour later. Peg thought, 'Good riddance!'

TWENTY-EIGHT

From the diary of Emma Schnee 3/3/1910. "It is three days since my beautiful baby Elizabeth, 'my bambina,' arrived. She is perfect. My Max he says, 'So tiny!' but he's a man. What do men know?

This happiness I would never have known without Dr. Smith. Such a kind and smart man. When my Max and I first came here I thought surely I was to die. But the Dr. he take my hand and say 'I will make you well with the magic cedar water. My dear you are going to live long and happy life'. I don't think I believe him then. I do now.

Some of the others in the sanatorium they say he is strange and talk about how he goes into the swamps every day to get the waters. Others think he goes to hide gold. My Max and me we just think he is wonderful."

"Oh, Kyle this is the kind of thing we've been looking for." It was Thursday, Thanksgiving morning and as Kyle made coffee and breakfast, Cynthia had been reading her great grandmothers diaries. "If only she would write about what he did with the waters. How he treated her."

"Yes. Hopefully we will find something helpful in those books. Come in the kitchen and eat, after which I'm going to go out and get the paper and we will settle down here for an entire day of research. Everything is closed today. Oh yah, Happy Thanksgiving, darling." He leaned down and kissed her.

"Happy Thanksgiving, Kyle. We don't have a turkey."

"Oh … I think we can live without one, don't you?" He took her in his arms and kissed her again.

"If I could live on your kisses, I think I would live forever. Breakfast smells really good. Bacon and eggs?"

"Yep, toast, coffee, and OJ too. Let's eat."

After they ate, Kyle went out to buy a paper. Cynthia took a shower and got into some clean clothes—black stirrup pants, white blouse with a dark gray pullover sweater, and gray ankle boots. She tied her hair back in a ponytail with a white velvet ribbon.

As she was coming down the stairs Kyle returned and said, "You look wonderful darling." He gathered her in his arms and just held her close for a moment. "You know it's really warming up out there. The snow is melting like all get out. Almost feels like spring. Hard to believe just a day or two ago it was so cold, and snowing the way it was."

"It's really warming up that much?"

"It is. It feels like 60 degrees outside. When I got the paper from the newsstand I saw Donna, the owner ... can't think of her last name ... doesn't matter. Anyway she told me they caught the guy that killed the woman whose body they found floating in the river after Halloween. Seems they were visiting from New York. She said the whole story is in today's paper, I read part of it."

"Did they ever find out who that poor woman was?"

"Well sort of. Apparently she was a dancer from New York. The only name they have for her so far is her stage name: Velvet Silkflower."

"Did it say why he killed her? People are so careless with their lives. They don't realize how precious life is. It makes me feel cold all over just to think about it. Hold me Kyle, please?" He took her in his arms and kissed the top of her head. After a few minutes she said. "I really don't want to read the paper. But I do want to read more in great grandma Emma's diaries."

They settled at the kitchen table with fresh coffee, Kyle with the paper and Cynthia with a diary from September 1909, paging through it, reading of day to day events that made up Emma's life. Emma got a new coat for the winter, was canning late summer vegetables, going for a walk in the beautiful sunshine with her Max after church on a Sunday. Then on September 27, "The letter Max sent with the money we owe William come back. Max says 'William is not at his old address anymore'. We are worried about him. We have not heard a word from him since last Christmas when he come to visit us. Where could he have gone to, and no tell us?"

"Oh, my God, Kyle. This is about the letter I found in Mom's house. The one that Max sent to William in New York that came back to them."

"The one with the gold coin?"

"Yes! This is so exciting. I feel I'm getting close to something."

"Maybe you should just try a book from an earlier year?"

"I wanted to but this one from 1909 is as far back as they go. Kyle are you sure you brought all the little trunks down from the attic?"

"Every one I could see. But if you like I'll go up and take another look around, just in case."

"Would you? I'm sure you looked, but would you check again?"

"Sure, where is that big three cell Maglite you have? I can look in all the little dark corners with that." He winked at her.

Ten minutes later he was in the attic. It looked just as empty and bleak as it did last night. Not quite as cold as it was then. Standing there looking around he heard the drip, drip, drip of water from the melting snow on the roof leaking in a dozen different places. The old cardboard boxes were just as he had left them. But wait! In the shadow behind the boxes he could see one last little steamer trunk someone had pushed into the far corner to support a cracked rafter. It was covered with mold and was wet from a leak right above it.

Kyle went downstairs and with out a word to Cynthia got several large pieces of fire wood from the backyard. As he was about to carry them upstairs Cynthia said. "What are you going to do with that? Make a fire in my attic?"

"Just be patient darling. I will be back in a few minutes with one last very nasty looking trunk." When he reached the attic he braced his back against the rafter and as he pushed up he stacked the fire wood to take the load from the little trunk. Then on hands and knees he grabbed the slimy handle and slid the trunk free. Next Kyle emptied one of the smaller cardboard boxes and used the cardboard to wrap the trunk so he could carry it downstairs.

He had just reached the living room when the doorbell rang. Cynthia smiled at him shook her head and went to answer the door. When she opened it, Peg and Ted were standing there. "Happy Thanksgiving!" they cried.

"Hi you guys! Happy Thanksgiving to you. What are you doing here? You should be with your families."

"We were at Mom and Dad's house and Peg suggested we see what you two are up to, and Mom said we should see if we could round you up and ask you to join us."

Kyle put down the trunk, came to the door and shook Ted's hand, hugged Peg and said, "Happy Thanksgiving! Peg what is this ring I see on your left hand?"

"It is an engagement ring. Ted asked me, and I said yes."

Cynthia and Peg squealed at the same time and hugged each other. Kyle shook Ted's hand again and said. "Congratulations, you dog you. When did this happen? Come on Ted spill …"

"Well, we were having Sunday brunch, and well … I asked her."

"So then when's the wedding?"

"In about two weeks, on the tenth. Ah, speaking of which we sort of have something to ask you and Cynthia. Will the two of you be our witnesses, maid of honor, and best man kind of thing?"

Kyle and Cynthia stared with open mouths. Peg looked at Ted and put a hand to her forehead. "That's part of what I love about him. He just barges ahead like a battering ram." Then she started to laugh.

They all started to laugh. When they had settled down a little, Cynthia asked, "He was joking, right?"

Peggy said, "Uh … no. Now that the cat is out of the bag so to speak, we really do want the two of you to stand for us."

Kyle said, "Whoa, in two weeks? How big a wedding are we talking here? I mean, Justice of the Peace? Maybe we could. Three hundred guests, formal, no way!"

"Much, much smaller than three hundred guests. Not quite just us and a judge," said Ted.

Cynthia said, "I know it's early, but I need a drink. Maybe even something stronger than a glass of wine. Please let's all sit down and get a grip on this thing."

"Look guys, come on in," said Kyle as he closed the door. "Let's sit and have a cup of coffee or something."

Peg said, "Sure Kyle, in the kitchen? Come on Ted."

They sat around the table in Cynthia's kitchen as water dripped into the buckets and pans. Peg and Ted told them about how they got engaged and the plans they had made for a very small wedding at the Renault winery. About twenty people and that would include the four of them.

Cynthia said, "What about dresses and things, flowers, pictures? "She was interrupted by Magic as he jumped into her lap. "Well Magic I guess you were feeling left out, weren't you?" She rubbed the kitty's head.

Peg reached over to scratch him too. "Magic? When did you name him? That's a really great name. It fits him."

"The other day. It just came to me because of the way he \pops up all of a sudden. Now about today, you're sure your mom wants us there? I mean, Thanksgiving is a family thing."

"Just stop right there, Cynthia," protested Ted. "Mom wouldn't invite you if she didn't mean it. Besides she has known Kyle forever and I know she and dad want to get to know you too. Especially if you are going to be in their son's wedding. Mom always makes enough food to feed an army anyway. Now whadya say? Everybody drink up and let's go. The turkey was really starting to smell good when Peg and I left."

Kyle said, "How about you guys go on and we'll get changed into some suitable clothes and meet you there in say, an hour or so?"

Peg and Ted looked at each other and nodded. Ted said, "Mom said the turkey would be ready at three. Its twelve thirty now so, yah, that'll work."

When they were gone, Cynthia turned to Kyle with a mischievous grin. "You realize you don't have any other clothes here, sir."

"I know. I thought while you shower and change, I could run home and maybe pack a little suitcase.

"Thinking of staying are you?"

He took her in his arms. "With you, darling, I'm thinking of staying forever."

She giggled and kissed him. "I miss you when you're gone from me—even for just a little while."

"You what Cynthia? Hell, I miss you when you're just in the other room." They hugged tighter and he kissed her again, this time the way she really liked him to. After a few minutes he pulled away. "I'll be back before you know it."

Then he was gone, out the door. Cynthia trudged up the steps, missing him already. 'Now what am I going to wear? I know! My red cowl-neck sweater and I'll put mom's green holly leaf pin on it. Kyle will like the way I look in that.' As she skipped up the last few steps a sharp pain stabbed her side. She gasped and sat down on the top step. Surprisingly, the pain left almost as fast as it had come. Standing carefully, Cynthia slowly and carefully made her way to her bedroom. Moving slowly she dressed in gray slacks, black low-heel boots and her red sweater. After fixing her make up and brushing her hair, she returned to the living room. No pain.

She was sitting on the couch with a glass of Merlot when Kyle returned. He was wearing tan Dockers, a burgundy-red long sleeved shirt and a black leather car coat. Cynthia thought he looked very handsome. "Hey sailor, you got a date for Thanksgiving?"

"As a matter of fact I do, and with a very beautiful lady." He set his suitcase down. She stood and stepped into his arms. "And you are she!"

"Oh just shut up and kiss me," she whispered. He did. Then again, and again. When he finally stopped, she was flushed and a little breathless. "WOW! Do you think we really have to go?"

"I do."

"I need to get you to say that again sometime in the future."

"I will. You name the time and place."

"Kyle, that almost sounds like a sneaky sort of marriage proposal?"

"Umm … you could take it that way."

"First them, now us. But I need to get well first."

"You will!"

"You are so very sure; you're just an optimist today, aren't you?"

"Yes I am. It is a beautiful day outside. Almost feels like May it's so warm. And best of all I have the most fantastic lady who I love very much, to take someplace special on this wonderful day. What do you think of that?"

"Spring fever!" she added cheerfully. "Oh, and Kyle? On our way is there someplace we can stop where they might sell cheap little earrings?"

"As a matter of fact, the newsstand where I got the paper this morning has a display of costume jewelry; you might find something there. I don't know just what they have or if it's what you are looking for, but I think it's the only thing open today that might. What is it you want?"

"I had a pair of small red plastic earrings. They kind of looked like little holly berries. I can't find them and I thought maybe …"

"Sure we can stop there on the way. It's just around the corner. But if we are going to stop, we'd better get going or we'll be late to Ted's parents' house."

A short time later in Kyle's Porsche, they stopped in front of "Donna's Stuff." Cynthia read the name of the store. Underneath the bright letters it said, "Newspapers, Magazines, & Stuff. She giggled. "The lady sells stuff?"

"Yes, she does! Come on, let's take a look around." In the tiny store, Cynthia was taken aback by the amount of "stuff" inside, especially the number of things from England and London in particular. An attractive blond woman dressed all in black leather was behind the counter. "Cynthia this is Donna, Donna, Cynthia Dobbs."

"Hi, Cynthia what can I get for you?"

"I need a pair of earrings that look like red holly berries. Have anything like that?"

"As a matter of fact, I have the cutest little holly leaves with berries. I got them in for the holidays and I think I have just one pair left."

Cynthia loved them as soon as she saw them. A few minutes later they were on their way to Thanksgiving dinner. "You know Kyle, she is a very pretty lady."

"Donna? Ya, she is very attractive. She opened that shop after her parents died. Her dad used to sell wholesale meats to the markets all over the south Jersey area. And, here is Ted's parent's house." He pulled into the driveway and parked behind Ted's car.

TWENTY-NINE

Early the next morning, which was known across the U.S. as 'Black Friday,' Kyle and Cynthia were in the living room of the old Stanton house. Sitting with a steaming cup of coffee, she watched as Kyle cleaned the slime from the last trunk and tried to get it open. "Looks like this has been wet for a long time and the wood is swollen. I can try to pry the top up but I think it will break."

"I don't care if it breaks. I just want to see if the older diaries are in there Kyle." She winced. "It really is a slimy mess isn't it?"

With the end of a screwdriver wedged in the crack between the lid and the body of the trunk, Kyle pressed down harder and harder on the handle of the screwdriver. Then slowly, with creaking and groaning, the top began to lift up. He got his fingers in there and lifted. The rusted hinges squealed in protest but the top was at last open. Looking inside Kyle said, "This is not good. The books are here but they are very wet. We'll have to be careful and try to dry them in someway to see if anything can be read from them."

Cynthia reached in and grabbed the top book. At the feel of the slimy wet leather she said, "Yuck!" But she didn't let go and carefully pulled it away from the next book down. It's back was stuck to the other book and it made a sucking sound as it came free. Holding the book in one hand she tried to open it with the other. The cover came away and exposed a solid block of wet pages. Looking closely, she couldn't even read the first page; the ink had smeared and soaked through the paper. "Kyle, this is hopeless. We'll never be able to read anything in these."

"We don't know that for sure. That's only one book. We'll just have to keep working on them. Maybe something can be saved."

She dropped the book on top of the others and it landed with a splat. Kyle took her in his arms. "It will be okay darling. Don't despair, Cynthia, please. We will fix this somehow." As she cried softly against his shoulder, she thought how safe and protected she always felt in Kyle's arms.

Even though it was fairly warm outside, it was chilly and damp in the house. Kyle built a fire in the fireplace and they worked together to remove all the books from the trunk. To their surprise and delight the books at the center of the box were nearly dry. They had been protected by the soft, wet leather of the outer volumes, sealing them in, and could be opened and read like any other books.

With trembling fingers, Cynthia lifted out one that said December 1907.

THIRTY

Peggy pulled her car into the nearest parking spot to the mall entrance. "You will love the dress I want. It's all white velvet and fur and ..."

"Yes, you have told me a thousand times. I'm sure it is the most perfect dress ever!"

"Cynthia, I'm sorry if I ramble on, but it is my wedding dress. I just know you'll like it, and we'll find the perfect dress for you as my maid of honor."

It was Monday, November twenty-ninth. Peg had picked up Cynthia to shop for a maid of honor dress, and go for a fitting of her wedding gown. "I'm sorry," said Cynthia, hiding a wince of pain by turning her head away, looking out her side window. "I'm just a little up-tight and shaky today. Maybe it's the excitement of looking for my dress. Please forgive me? You know I want you and Ted to have the greatest wedding ever. Where did you say the shop is?"

"It's called 'Susie's Bridal Boutique' and it's on the second level."

As they walked into the mall Cynthia suddenly grabbed her abdomen and bent over in pain.

"Cynthia! What's wrong? You're white as a ghost. Here let me help you we'll sit on this bench for a bit." They sat down. "Are you okay? What is it?"

"I, I have pain ... it'll pass in a bit if I just rest for a little while. Look, there's a coffee shop. If we go sit there and I have a cup of tea and a glass of water I can take a pain pill and I'll be okay."

"You're sure you don't want me to call 911 or something? You look so pale." Cynthia shook her head and after a few minutes they got up and with Peggy's help found seats in the back of the coffee shop.

After Cynthia took her pill, and they sat there for some time, Peg said, "Your color is coming back a bit. How do you feel?"

"Better, better ... I guess I should explain what this is all about, huh?" She gave Peg a weak smile and sipped her tea.

"Are you ill? Or pregnant or something? You scared the bejesus out of me just now. If you're sick, got the flu or some such thing we can do this another day. Cynthia what's going on?"

"Well, please don't be too shocked. But the short answer is ... that I'm dying."

Peggy sat there with her mouth open for a full minute. "Dying? You mean like dying to marry Kyle, or to buy a new dress, or ... or ... DYING in capitals? You mean as in dead. End of life dying? You can't be! You look so healthy, I mean you're a little thin ... but dying? Okay, tell me. I can handle it. If I could get through losing Tim, I can handle anything." She took a deep breath and slowly shook her head. "Even my new best friend saying some shit like she's dying."

"Oh, Peg it's ... it's. I have a disease called Secondary Amyloidosis, S.A. for short. It's a bit complicated to explain all about it but I'm in the end stages. You don't survive this thing that I have. I came here to look for a cure that Dr. Smith might have used on my great grandmother back in 1906. However, I haven't even been able to find out for sure if she had S.A. or not."

"This S.A.—how long have you had it? What does it do to you? Don't they have some kind of treatment to fix it? Is it like AIDS? What? Come on Cyn ... spill. I never heard of this S.A stuff."

"Stuff, yeah, that's a good description of what it is. This stuff, amyloid. It builds up in the organs of the body. When enough is built up they stop working and you die. The treatments they have only slow it down. When they stop slowing it, the end is not far away."

"And you had the treatments? Now they don't work anymore?"

"That's right. My doctor, Dr. Hicks, tells me I have only a very short time."

"Cynthia this is terrible! Here I am going on about my wedding and you ... you, oh my God! Isn't there anything anyone can do?"

"They say not. But I had hoped to find a cure in the museum records. Only it seems there are no records—none that will help me anyway. Kyle and I have found my great grandmother's diaries and I thought there might be something in them. But there are only hints and a few words about tonics and things. Nothing about how they were made or worked or were used. I still don't know if she even had S.A. or something entirely different."

"What about another doctor? Have you had a second opinion? Maybe this Dr. Hicks is just wrong."

"In the beginning I got several opinions. As you might imagine it was pretty hard to accept that I had an incurable disease. They all said the same thing. I've searched everything in libraries on the Internet ... everywhere. There is nothing. My only last hope was to find something here in Egg Harbor City, but so far, nothing.

"I do feel much better now. How about we go look at this fantastic dress of yours, and see if we can find something for me?"

As they entered the Bridal Boutique, a lovely dark haired lady came up to them, and with a slight French accent said. "Peggy! You have come to try on your dress? Just this morning Nanette finished the alterations."

"Susie, this is Cynthia. Cynthia, Susie. Yes, I have come for my fitting, and Cynthia is to be my Maid of Honor, so we need to find a dress for her."

"Very well. While you go with Nanette and get fitted with your dress, I will show Cynthia the most beautiful gown in green velvet with white fur trim that there has ever been."

Peggy went with Nanette and Susie led Cynthia to the far corner of the shop, where a most lovely green velvet sheath style dress with fur trim was on display. Cynthia exclaimed, "It has tiny gold roses in the white fur neckline. Do they match the ones Peg has been telling me are on her dress?"

"Just so. Hers are around the waist and yours are on the fur neckline and cuffs. What do you think? Would you like to try it on? I think it is just about your size."

Cynthia touched the fur trim; it was so very soft. The neckline came out to the top of the shoulder and the green velvet sleeves came to the wrist where they were trimmed in white fur with tiny gold roses worked onto the point of trim that came out on the back of the hand. "Yes I would. Where are the dressing rooms?"

Removing the dress from the manikin Susie said, "Right this way."

Twenty minutes later as Cynthia stepped out of the dressing room door, she almost ran into Peggy. They looked at each other, giggled, then hugged, then almost cried. "My God, Peggy. You look wonderful!"

"And look at you. I love that green velvet. Oh, my God it has the tiny gold roses to match my dress!" They hugged again then looked at themselves in the mirrors. "You know ... what we need now is shoes!"

THIRTY-ONE

Kyle and Ted were at the Old Bay bar and grill. They'd been there most of the afternoon. It started with lunch, and then they stayed to have a few with some of the guys. Most everybody had left but them. "You know Kyle, you seem kind of glum lately. You got trouble with Cynthia or something?"

"Yeah—or something. Ted can I confide in you? You won't tell Peg or anybody?"

Feeling good that an older guy like Kyle wanted to confide in him, Ted said, "You can trust me buddy. I don't tell no one nothing'. Whatcha got? Lay it on me, big guy."

So Kyle told him about Cynthia and the S.A. And the damn, wet diaries and how they had tried everything they could think of to dry them so they would be readable.

"Dying! Cynthia … dying? Oh, man—that's heavy. Damn and she looks so hot too." Kyle looked at him with raised eyebrows. "No offense man, I mean she looks healthy you know, not sick or anything. You really think you can find a cure from a hundred years ago to fix her today? Damn, that would be somethin."

They sat drinking for a while in silence, each with his own thoughts. "You know Kyle, Mark works with the state crime lab. He told me one time that they have a way to remove moisture from documents without hurting them."

"How?"

"I don't know, you'd have to ask him."

Before Ted could finish his beer, Kyle threw a hundred on the bar and was dragging him out the door. "Whoa, Kyle what's the rush? Where are we going?"

"Do you know where Mark works? Or his office number?"

"I have his cell."

"Call him. Find out if we can see him today. Now!"

A short time later and forty miles away, they walked into Mark's office at the state crime lab. After they explained what they wanted, Mark said, "If you will bring me the documents I can dry them in a freezing vacuum chamber. What I'll do is freeze them then put them in a special chamber and pump out all the air. The moisture goes directly from frozen to water vapor without ever being a liquid. It takes a while but the documents will be dry as bone when I take them out."

Kyle asked, "Could you do that for me, ASAP?"

"If the chamber isn't being used, I can start the process tomorrow. Depending on how much material you have, it could take several weeks."

"That long? Damn. But I guess it's better than anything else I've got going. Thanks Mark."

That evening Kyle dropped the three oldest wet diaries off at Mark's house. After looking them over, Mark said, "I think maybe ten days to two weeks to dry them. I checked and you're in luck—the chamber is not being used. I can start processing them when I go into work tomorrow."

THIRTY-TWO

During the week before the wedding Cynthia had been having more frequent and stronger attacks of pain. Three days before the wedding, Kyle found her doubled over on a kitchen chair clutching her stomach. "Cynthia! Should I call 911? I've never seen you in such pain."

"No Kyle, it's just I can't get up stairs for my pain pills. Would you be a dear and get me two? They're in the top drawer of the nightstand."

"Two? I thought you were only supposed to take one at a time."

"I am, but for the last few days I've needed two to get the pain under control. Please Kyle, get them for me? And Kyle, you know better than to call 911. When my time comes it won't be an emergency."

Frowning, Kyle ran upstairs and was back a few minutes later with two pills and a glass of water. "Thank you, sweetheart." She straightened slowly to an upright sitting position, with a grimace of pain on her face. After taking the pills she bent over again. Kyle rubbed her back. He didn't know what to say, so he watched and waited patiently for more than half an hour until Cynthia lifted her head and said, "It's better now. Can you help me to the living room? I think I'll lie on the couch and rest for a while."

He offered his hand to help her up. She hugged him and rested her head on his chest. "Kyle, my darling man, whatever would I have done if I hadn't found you? I owe you so much and now with your help, my last wishes are expressed in the living will your lawyer David drew up for me."

"No need to worry about last wishes. We are going to get you well. We're going to find a cure for this thing that's trying to take you from me. Now let's get you into the living room so you can have a rest."

After she was settled on the couch, Magic jumped up and sat next to her. She scratched the kitty's head. "Good Magic. Mama's baby." Her cell phone rang. "Would you get that Kyle? It's on the kitchen table."

Kyle answered the phone. It was Mark telling him he had been trying to reach him because the books were dry and Kyle could pick them up any time.

"Cynthia! Great news! Mark says the books are done. You rest and I'll run over to Mark's and pick them up. Maybe when I get back you'll feel good enough so we can look at them together." He kneeled by the couch and ran his fingers gently through her hair. She smiled up at him. "I'll be right back sweetheart. You rest." He kissed her.

"I will be right here waiting for you to come back, sir."

He kissed her again, stood and went to the door. "I'll be back so quick you won't even know I'm gone."

"I'll know anyway. Hurry darling."

Twenty minutes later when he returned, Cynthia was asleep. He made a small fire in the fireplace and sitting on the floor next to the couch with a glass of wine he started to read the oldest of Emma's diaries. He was startled a short time later when Cynthia put her hand on the back of his neck. "Find anything of interest?"

"Hello, sleepy head. As a matter of fact I have, listen to this from December 1906: 'It was most strange today. I was to see the Dr., but when I come to his office his nurse is not there and I surprise him, walking in alone. He closed a big book so quick like he is hiding something. But not like he was reading but putting something in. He said for me to go out and wait. He is not so sharp with me most times.'

Kyle looked up from the pages and smiled just a bit. Makes you wonder if the old boy was caught by your great-grandma doing something sneaky."

"Sneaky as in …?"

"I don't know, my love. But it was something. It looks like he had his secrets too, and after all, they are what we're looking for."

They spent the rest of the day going through the books. Peg called to tell them everything was ready at Renault's for the wedding at nine am on Saturday. The weather was supposed to remain unseasonably warm until the weekend, when according to the forecast it was going to get much colder, with the possibility of snow.

THIRTY-THREE

Early Saturday morning, Cynthia felt very well for a change. The weather was sunny, but with a cold northwest wind blowing. She and Kyle arrived at the winery about seven thirty. Peg and Cynthia went to the bride's room to get dressed, while Kyle and Ted found a seat in the coffee shop before getting into their tuxedos. A little small talk later, it was time.

At five minutes to nine, with about fifteen guests seated in the small winery hall where the tours normally started, Ted and Kyle took their places with the justice of the peace. Right on time, Cynthia appeared in the doorway. The music started, and as she glided down the aisle, Kyle thought she was the most beautiful woman he had ever seen. In the green velvet dress, with the white fur trim accenting her lovely neck and shoulders, she looked like a Christmas Angel, his Snow Angel. She carried a bouquet of white carnations at her waist. Reaching the men, she took her place opposite Kyle.

Then Peggy was coming down the aisle, and everyone stood. She was the perfect Christmas bride in her white velvet gown. She wore a veil which dropped down her back all the way to the floor. Just below the hemline they could see white pumps sparkling like fresh snow in sunshine on a winter's morning.

She was escorted by her father. When they reached the end of the aisle and the justice of the peace asked, "Who giveth this woman?" the first pain started in Cynthia's stomach. She gritted her teeth and hoped it wouldn't get worse. By the time he said, "I now pronounce you man and wife," she was beginning to bend forward and clutch the bouquet tightly against her abdomen. And when he said,

"You may now kiss the bride," black spots were telling Cynthia she was passing out.

As Ted took Peggy in his arms and kissed his new bride for the first time, Kyle was in motion. In two long strides he crossed behind the kissing couple and caught Cynthia in his arms as she crumpled to the floor. Lifting her gently, he carried her up the aisle where only a short time before she had looked so beautiful walking down.

He didn't stop for people who offered assistance; he didn't stop at the doors, but pushed his way through. He didn't stop until he reached his car and placed Cynthia gently in the passenger seat. As he tore down the road to the hospital, his Porsche left two long black streaks on the pavement.

Half an hour later, still in their wedding clothes, Peg and Ted joined Kyle in the emergency room. Ted asked, "How is she Kyle?"

"I don't know. She was unconscious when we got here. They took her down there." He waved vaguely in the direction of the exam rooms. "She was so pale … I carried her in here and kissed her and told her it would be okay. She didn't hear me and they took her away. I gave them her information at the desk. But they wouldn't tell me anything … I … I…."

Peg sat down next to him and put her arm around his shoulders. "She'll be okay, Kyle I just know she will."

"No. She won't. They can't do much of anything for her except ease her pain. She is near the end and she has a DNR on file that her doctor's office is faxing. At this point, even if there was a way to treat the disease, they can only make her comfortable. They understand that she's terminal." He choked out the final words as tears rolled down his face.

Two hours later, a doctor named Schmitt approached Kyle and told him Cynthia had been admitted and moved to a room. She was awake and they could go up to visit.

As they entered the cold white hospital room, Cynthia was on the bed. Machines beeping and blinking around her. There was an IV in her arm and she looked very pale, but awake and she smiled upon seeing them. She said, "Peg, Ted I am so sorry … I…."

Peg sat on the edge of the bed and said, "Hey you, it's okay. You ready to blow this place and come dance at our reception? You stole the show you know. You're not supposed to upstage the bride."

Kyle touched Peg's arm and she moved so he could sit by Cynthia. Cynthia tilted her head up to receive his kiss. He whispered, "I love you Cyn. We'll have you up and outta here before you know it. Then we are going to find the cure that fixed your great-grandma."

"You know, Kyle, I've been thinking. In her diaries she said it looked like he hid something in a book when she walked in on him. Do you think it could have been 'The Doctor's Book' that you have on display in the museum?"

"You know, it could be. Nobody has tried to open it and look through it because of its fragile condition. As soon as we get you home, you and I are going to take a very close look at that book."

A short time later Peg and Ted left to see about their guests at the reception. Kyle sat with Cynthia. They watched TV and he was reading a newspaper article about the market's big rise when he noticed that her eyes were closed. 'Napping' he thought, 'Good, she needs to rest.'

About two in the afternoon a nurse came in to check Cynthia's vital signs. He was unable to wake her. Dr. Schmitt was called and after examining Cynthia he said she had slipped into a coma.

Kyle exclaimed, "She can't be comatose, she's just sleeping. Are you sure doctor? She was talking to me just a little while ago."

"I'm sorry, Kyle but she is. I don't think it's a very deep coma and she could snap out of it anytime. Of course because of the DNR there isn't a lot we can do. I would suggest you and any other friends or relatives she has sit and talk to her as much as possible. Sometimes it helps them wake up."

"We will. Thank you, doctor ..." Kyle sat by her bed and held Cynthia's hand. As the doctor and nurse left the room, Kyle started to tell Cynthia how very much he loved and needed her. Would she please come back to him? He needed her so very much.

Many hours later, Peg and Ted came to visit again. They were shocked and saddened when Kyle told them about the coma. They both agreed Kyle should go home and get some rest. They would stay with Cynthia.

Kyle had been gone about five hours. Peg was sitting by the bed telling Cynthia about the reception and how concerned everyone was, when Cynthia opened her eyes and said, "Where's Kyle? He was here just a minute ago."

"Cynthia, you're awake! Oh, thank God!"

"Why? Was I asleep a long time? Where is Kyle anyway? And what time is it? Oh, hi Ted; I didn't see you sitting over there. What's going on?"

"Hi, Cynthia. Glad you're back with us. You gave everybody a real scare. Kyle went home to get a little rest. We chased him away by promising to stay with you. It's been a long time. You were in a coma. I'll call Kyle right away and tell him you're awake."

"A coma! It seemed like I just dozed off. How long has it been?"

"You were out about twelve hours sweetie. It's after midnight. Ted and I have been here since about seven."

"What day is it?"

"It's still Saturday. No wait, it's Sunday now. You want some water or anything?"

"Yes. Oh, isn't this your wedding night? Oh damn, I really spoiled it all didn't I? Oh, shit Peg. Ted, I'm so sorry."

"It's okay, Cynthia, you just get well. Ted, why don't you go tell the nurse or somebody that she's awake. Then call Kyle. I'll sit here with her till you get back."

When Ted was gone, Peg leaned in close to Cynthia and said, "I have some news that will really wake you up. Wanna hear it?"

"What now? Oh, no ... did I spoil something else?"

"No silly ... I'm pregnant."

"Really? When did you know? How far along are you? Does Ted know? Come on spill. You can't drop a bombshell like that on me and just leave it hanging."

Well, you remember when I was so long in the bathroom this morning in the dressing room? I took a home pregnancy test. I thought for a month maybe I was, but you know how it can be. You're sleeping with somebody and you miss and then you get it and you think safe for another month. Well this time the curse didn't come, and so I thought I didn't want to get married not knowing. Anyway, Ted doesn't know. I'm going to spring it on him on our wedding night and see how he holds up, if you know what I mean. So, how about that? At thirty-nine I'm going to have a baby.

Cynthia leaned up and hugged Peg. "It's wonderful. And you're right about one thing; I sure am wide awake now! Man, a wedding and a baby all in one day."

"Well, it's not like I've had it yet. I'm probably about six weeks along. I'll go see a doctor when we come back from our honeymoon."

"Oh, my God! You guys are supposed to leave for Las Vegas tomorrow, I mean today ... now, oh shit ... I've messed that up too, haven't I?"

"Not to worry Cyn. We can go another time or get a later flight or something. Right now we need to get you well and back on your feet."

The nurse came in and asked Peg to move away from the bed so she could check Cynthia's vital signs. "Do you know just what time she woke up?"

"About half an hour ago I guess. Is it important?"

"The doctor will want to know in the morning. I just need to note it on her chart."

Ted came back and said, "Kyle is on his way."

Cynthia said, "Now that will really make me feel better."

The nurse said, "With all the pain medication you're getting you should feel great. Open your eyes very wide and follow my finger with them. Very good. Are you hungry? Okay folks, I'll be back in a little while with some light food for her."

"Look, you guys, I'm better now and it's not like I'm ever really going to get better than I am, so why don't you see if you can get to the airport and take that honeymoon? You should be able to make it. Your flight is what eight this morning? And it's what one? That gives you more than six hours."

"Look Cynthia, Ted and I can't just fly off and leave you here in the hospital. I wouldn't feel right about it."

"No, Peg. Kyle will be here soon. I'll be okay. You know what they say 'You never get out of life alive.' I've had this thing for a long time, and we all know how it will end. So you go. Enjoy your honeymoon. I'll be all right."

"Well, we could make the flight, Peg. Cynthia does have a point. What do you think?

Shall we give it a try?"

"Please do," pleaded Cynthia with a weak smile.

With renewed excitement rising in her voice Peggy said, "If you're sure Cyn, we'll make a run for it."

"I'm sure. You guys go have a great time. Send me a postcard. I will be here waiting to hear all about it next week when you get back. Now, go."

They both hugged her and said they would call to check on her and see her next week. When they were gone Cynthia lay back exhausted, she slipped into a light doze, and then a much deeper, healing sleep.

Next thing she knew there were soft lips on hers, kissing her awake. Kyle was sitting on the edge of the bed. "Hey, Sleeping Beauty. You know you have the most beautiful eyes I have ever seen?"

"I bet you say that to all your girlfriends, don't you Kyle?"

"Only the one I'm in love with." She smiled, and he kissed her again. "I wouldn't have waked you but they will be bringing your breakfast soon. So, I thought as much as I like to watch you sleep, I love looking into your eyes even more. So, like Prince Charming, I kissed my Sleeping Beauty awake. Now we have a few minutes together in peace before they come to feed you."

"Breakfast, what time is it? It seems like Peg and Ted just left."

"It is six a.m. my dear. I've been sitting here reading and watching you since about one thirty. How do you feel this morning?"

"I don't seem to have any pain, but I'm very tired. Though that might be the pain meds they have me on."

Later Dr. Schmitt came to check on her and said if she felt up to it she could go home, as there was nothing they could do to improve her condition. He would prescribe a stronger pain medication she could take.

About noon they were very surprised when Peg and Ted walked into the room. Cynthia said, "What are you guys doing here?"

Peg said, "We were at the airport. It's a mad house. There is this huge storm down south and flights all across the country are delayed or canceled. Ours was one of the canceled ones, because we connect through Atlanta. We decided since we were flying first class, and the tickets are refundable, we would postpone our honeymoon a week or two. Ted called the hotel in Vegas, since we were in the honeymoon suite, and you all know how much I like to play at their casino here in Atlantic City. Well, they kind of comped us an extra night if we would come the first week in January, as long as it's after January second."

"Why January second? And what huge storm?"

"January second because the first and New Years are always packed in Vegas. But the week after is always on the slow side. And the storm! Well, don't you watch the news? A few days ago they were saying we might get a little snow on Sunday. Now it's Sunday and they are saying this is going to be a huge nor'easter. We're going to get lots of snow in the next few days. Strong winds—the whole thing. Big storm. It's supposed to start tonight. Another reason Ted and I decided to postpone. We want to be here with our families and our friends."

Kyle said, "If it's gonna snow like that and be really bad it's a good thing they are letting you go home this afternoon."

Peg said, "They're letting you go home? That's wonderful. Are you better? I thought ..."

"It's okay Peg. No I'm not better as in 'well,' but I'm taking a bed from someone who might get well. I'm good enough to go home for a while longer. Or they think so anyway. With S.A. you never know."

Later that day as she was dressing in clothes Kyle had brought to the hospital, Cynthia suddenly put her hand to her forehead and collapsed on the floor. Kyle lifted her to the bed. When he couldn't wake her, he rang for the nurse.

In the evening, Peg and Ted were sitting in the visitor's chairs. Kyle and Dr. Schmitt were standing by the bed. Dr. Schmitt said, "She's in a coma again; it seems to be a deeper one this time."

Kyle asked, "How can she go in and out like this? What causes something like that? She's fine one minute and in a coma the next. This is crazy."

"Well, her organs are so hard and gummed up that they try to shut down. In reaction to this her body goes in a deep sleep, a coma, which lets her survive on a minimal amount of energy and organ function. She may slip in and out for sometime before the end. Sometimes patients with this condition rally and go for hours or days between comas. But eventually she will not wake up from one and die. There's nothing anyone can do or try. You know that."

"Well, there's something I can try!" Kyle raised his fisted hands, shaking them at the ceiling and shouted, "Cynthia I will find that spring and the secret of saving you, I swear it!" He ran from the room to the elevators, pressed, pressed, and pressed the button. Out of patience, he ran down the emergency stairs, through the lobby, and out the front doors, into the dark and the snow that was just beginning to fall.

THIRTY-FOUR

On the other side of town, Carol got a phone call that her mother had had a heart attack and was in a hospital in Philadelphia. She and Stan got into their car and backed out of the garage and into a very heavy snowfall that had already covered the ground. "Go slow, Stan. I want to get to mother fast, but I do want to get there in one piece."

At the museum the snow was blowing and starting to drift against the building as Kyle's Porsche slid to a halt at the curb. He went in, turned off the alarm and turned on all the lights. He stood in front of the display case by the front door, staring at 'The Doctor's Book.' It was a cherished and fragile artifact from the past, and he knew it would feel wrong to touch it.

He opened the back of the case slowly. The book was big, eight inches thick, heavy, and very fragile. Kyle slid it slowly back from the shelf, carefully easing it onto the palm of his right hand. He lifted it free of the case and as he turned his foot caught in the hem of an old wool bathing costume that was on display. He stumbled a step forward, then lost his balance and fell to his knees. The book slipped from his fingers, and crashed to the floor. Thousands of fragile pages scattered like autumn leaves. "No!" he cried as his hands reached out too far, making him lose his balance yet again. He fell forward and hit his head on the concrete floor. Blackness enveloped him.

The snow fell heavily outside. Deepening, blowing, drifting, it covered the world in deep folds of white. The temperature fell: 25, 20, 15 …

*   *   *   *

Kyle awakened in darkness. The power was off. He shivered in the cold. Stumbling, he groped around and found the switch for the emergency lights. They were dim, but some light nevertheless. He went back and sat on the floor by the scattered pages. "I've failed you Cynthia. How can I find anything in this pile?"

In despair he picked up the front cover which was stiff and hard in his hands. He could feel the edges crumble. There was a lump on what would be the inside cover. He peered closely in the dim light. There was something under the paper backing. With his fingernail he slit the edge open. There were thin pages inside a paper pocket. Pulling them out, he discovered a steppingstone path map that he clearly recognized as the grounds of the old sanatorium. With the map were two handwritten pages.

In trembling hands he read the formula for a 'cedar-water elixir'. According to the instructions it must be water from a certain spring that bubbled from the top of a pile of bog iron rocks in the middle of a small pond. But the map showed where the pond was and he knew it was still there.

Kyle rushed from the museum, brushed snow off the windshield with a sleeve and got into his car. At the corner he made a sliding turn onto Claudius Street and stopped by the bridge near the Egg Harbor City Water Works. He knew that the original was built in ... he couldn't remember. 'I should know when,' he thought, and shook his head. He stumbled down the embankment next to the stream. Union Creek was close to where Dr. Smith had fallen in 1859.

The snow was inches deep, but light and powdery. On all fours, Kyle scrambled around, feeling under the snow and years of fallen leaves, searching for the first stepping stone on the map. Not finding it, he stood up and studied the map in shaking, cold hands. Snowflakes dampened the paper. He was in the right place. 'Maybe this one spring ... so close to the road, has been lost over time.'

Kyle lurched through the snow, and followed the stream under overhanging cedar trees where the snow wasn't as deep. He searched again. Yes! A round stepping stone greeted his probing fingers. 'If only enough of them remain for me to follow the path.'

Trudging forward, groping on his hands and knees, Kyle pushed his cold, stiff, bleeding fingers through the snow and leaf litter, making slow progress. Suddenly the path ended in a frozen side stream. His hands slid out on the ice under the snow. 'No! No! It can't end here!'

He stood and looked all around. Big white flakes obscure his vision. 'Wait, what is that? It looks like a white cat on the far shore.' Kyle slipped and slid across the ice-covered stream. 'No cat. Just a trick of the snow and wind.'

He flopped down and sat on the steep bank. 'So tired, so very cold.' His hands were leaving crimson streaks in the white snow. He laid back and bumped his head on something under the snow. Kyle scrambled around and found a stepping stone on end, sticking up from the ground. 'Yes this must be the way.' He climbed the steep embankment. On reaching the top he found big, very old cedar trees grown tightly together all along the crest. 'No way through.'

Kyle worked his way along the line of cedar trees until he found one that had died and fallen. Stepping through the gap he saw a perfectly circular pond about fifty yards across, and in the middle, through the falling snow he could just make out a pile of snow-covered rocks with a spring of water bubbling from its top.

"Yes, yes. This must be it!" he shouted. He slid down the slope and out onto the snow-covered ice. Kyle heard it groan and creak and knew from years of skating on the Egg Harbor City Lake as a boy that the noise meant the ice might not be thick enough to hold him.

Carefully he worked his way toward the pile of rock. He pulled the old army canteen that he'd brought from the museum from his belt. The notes said he must get the cedar water before it hit the rocks—pure from the spring.

Reaching forward, concentrating on getting the water, Kyle was shocked when the ice under him gave a loud crack and he plunged into the deep, freezing pond water. Kicking upward he realized that he was under the ice and while it broke easily from above, it was as hard as rock from underneath.

A weak current pushed him along. He struggled and swam, trying again and again to surface, but to no avail.

*   *   *   *

Out on the highway as a car slid sideways past them, Carol told Dr. Stan, "Go slower! You'll kill us both. Thank God mama didn't really have a heart attack, but a tachycardia event. Who knew she had that? God, what a night! Watch out!"

"Carol, darling. Please ... I'm doing the best I can. Maybe we should turn into Egg Harbor on Heidelberg Avenue and go around past the museum to the house. On the side roads there won't be so many idiots on the road. We're almost home."

"Well, whatever you think is best. You're driving! Sort of."

Stan turned onto Heidelberg and then onto Claudius. As they approached the intersection with London Avenue, where the museum was just visible through the snow, Stan said, "What's that? Up ahead on the left."

They passed a car parked on the left side of the road, covered with snow. Carol said, "That's Kyle's Porsche. Keep going Stan. He's with that witch. I just know they're up to no good. Oh, just get us home Stan, please!"

It was the last chance Kyle had to be saved. Less then a hundred yards from the road as Carol said, "just get us home Stan, please!" Kyle was under the ice. He knew his time was running out by the pain in his lungs and the black spots closing in on his eyes. His last thoughts before the darkness took him were of Cynthia and the way she looked the first time he saw her—coming in through the museum door with snow in her hair—his snow angel.

THIRTY-FIVE

At the hospital, Cynthia's eyes fluttered open. Peg said, "There's my girl, back again. Look, she's awake, Dr. Schmitt. What's she saying Ted?"

Cynthia looked around as if she didn't know where she was. As if she was in another place. She said, "Kyle? Kyle ..." and in a whispery, fading voice, "I love you Kyle."

An hour later Dr. Schmitt said she was gone.

EPILOG

On Christmas morning as Donna was opening the newsstand for two hours of morning paper sales before closing for the holiday, she found a small, skinny white cat by the door. Having lost her big black cat 'Middy" just six months before, and after fourteen years and many oaths claiming 'no more pets,' Magic melted her heart. He found a new home with newspapers, good food, and love, as well as a new name—Snowstorm, quickly shortened to Snow.

Kyle's body was recovered in the January thaw. On a beautiful April day, Peg and Ted held what was supposed to be a small ceremony on the beach at the Egg Harbor City Lake. They were there to privately spread Kyle and Cynthia's ashes to the wind, the sand and the water, but nearly two hundred people came to say good-bye.

In May, the old Stanton place was sold to a young couple who loved Victorian style houses. They restored it and lived a long and full family life there with five children and in all that time never heard a whisper of a ghost or witch.

The Egg Harbor City Historical Society and Museum were well taken care of from Kyle's estate and the trust he had arranged.

On a bright summer morning in July, Peggy gave birth to a big, ten pound baby boy. Peggy and Ted named him Kyle C. to honor their lost friends.

The museum is there for you to visit. The serpentine stream sparkles in the summer sun. And the stepping stone paths, gold coins and magic spring remain secrets of the museum.

THE END

978-0-595-47718-0
0-595-47718-6

Printed in the United States
123971LV00010B/83/P